PROPERTY OF

_____

_____

E. B. WHITE was born in Mount Vernon, New York. He graduated from Cornell University in 1921, then travelled about trying many sorts of jobs, and finally joined the *New Yorker* magazine. He kept animals on his farm in Maine, and some of these creatures crept into his stories and books. In 1970 Mr White received the Laura Ingalls Wilder Award, given every five years for substantial and lasting contributions to children's literature by the American Library Association.

E. B. White died in 1985.

Books by E. B. White

CHARLOTTE'S WEB

STUART LITTLE

THE TRUMPET OF THE SWAN

E. B. WHITE

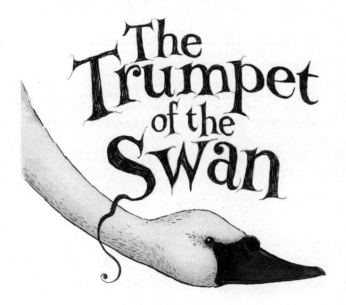

The Trumpet of the Swan

Illustrated by Edward Frascino

A PUFFIN BOOK

PUFFIN BOOKS

Published by the Penguin Group
Penguin Books Ltd, 80 Strand, London WC2R ORL, England
Penguin Group (USA) Inc., 375 Hudson Street, New York, New York 10014, USA
Penguin Group (Canada), 90 Eglinton Avenue East, Suite 700, Toronto, Ontario, Canada M4P 2Y3
(a division of Pearson Penguin Canada Inc.)
Penguin Ireland, 25 St Stephen's Green, Dublin 2, Ireland (a division of Penguin Books Ltd)
Penguin Group (Australia), 707 Collins Street, Melbourne, Victoria 3008, Australia
(a division of Pearson Australia Group Pty Ltd)
Penguin Books India Pvt Ltd, 11 Community Centre, Panchsheel Park, New Delhi – 110 017, India
Penguin Group (NZ), 67 Apollo Drive, Rosedale, Auckland 0632, New Zealand
(a division of Pearson New Zealand Ltd)
Penguin Books (South Africa) (Pty) Ltd, Block D, Rosebank Office Park,
181 Jan Smuts Avenue, Parktown North, Gauteng 2193, South Africa

Penguin Books Ltd, Registered Offices: 80 Strand, London WC2R ORL, England

puffinbooks.com

First published in the USA by Harper & Row, Publishers, Inc., New York, 1970
First published in Great Britain by Hamish Hamilton Children's Books Ltd, 1970
Published by Puffin Books 1993
Reissued in this edition 2014
001

Set in 13.5/20.5pt Sabon LT Std
Typeset by Jouve (UK), Milton Keynes
Printed in Great Britain by Clays Ltd, St Ives plc

British Library Cataloguing in Publication Data
A CIP catalogue record for this book is available from the British Library

ISBN: 978-0-141-35484-2

www.greenpenguin.co.uk

Contents

1. Sam

WALKING back to camp through the swamp, Sam wondered whether to tell his father what he had seen.

'I know *one* thing,' he said to himself. 'I'm going back to that little pond again tomorrow. And I'd like to go alone. If I tell my father what I saw today, he will want to go with me. I'm not sure that's a very good idea.'

Sam was eleven. His last name was Beaver. He was strong for his age and had black hair and dark eyes like an Indian. Sam walked like an Indian, too, putting one foot straight in front of the other and making very little noise. The swamp through which he was travelling was a wild place – there was no trail, and it was boggy underfoot, which made walking difficult. Every four or five minutes Sam took his compass out of his pocket and checked his course to make sure he was headed in a westerly direction. Canada is a big place. Much of it is wilderness. To get lost in the woods and swamps of western Canada would be a serious matter.

As he trudged on, the boy's mind was full of the wonder of what he had seen. Not many people in the world have seen the nest of a Trumpeter Swan. Sam had found one on the lonely pond on this day in spring. He had seen the two great white birds with their long white necks and black bills. Nothing he had ever seen before in all his life had made him feel quite the way he felt, on that wild little pond, in the presence of those two enormous swans. They were so much bigger than any bird he had ever seen before. The nest was big, too – a mound of sticks and grasses. The female was sitting on eggs; the male glided slowly back and forth, guarding her.

When Sam reached camp, tired and hungry, he found his father frying a couple of fish for lunch.

'Where have *you* been?' asked Mr Beaver.

'Exploring,' replied Sam. 'I walked over to a pond about a mile and a half from here. It's the one we see from the air as we're coming in. It isn't much of a place – nowhere near as big as this lake we're on.'

'Did you see anything over there?' asked his father.

'Well,' said Sam, 'it's a swampy pond with a lot of reeds and cattails. I don't think it would be any good for fishing. And it's hard to get to – you have to cross a swamp.'

'See anything?' repeated Mr Beaver.

'I saw a muskrat,' said Sam, 'and a few red-winged blackbirds.'

Mr Beaver looked up from the wood stove, where the fish were sizzling in a pan.

'Sam,' he said, 'I know you like to go exploring. But don't forget – these woods and marshes are not like the country around home in Montana. If you ever go over to that pond again, be careful you don't get lost. I don't like you crossing swamps. They're treacherous. You could step into a soggy place and get bogged down, and there wouldn't be anybody to pull you out.'

'I'll be careful,' said Sam. He knew perfectly well he would be going back to the pond where the swans were. And he had no intention of getting lost in the woods. He felt relieved that he had not told his father about seeing the swans, but he felt queer about it, too. Sam was not a sly boy, but he was odd in one respect: he liked to keep things to himself. And he liked being alone, particularly when he was in the woods. He enjoyed the life on his father's cattle ranch in the Sweet Grass country in Montana. He loved his mother. He loved Duke, his cow pony. He loved riding the range. He loved watching the guests who came to board at the Beavers' ranch every summer.

But the thing he enjoyed most in life was these camping trips in Canada with his father. Mrs Beaver didn't care for the woods, so she seldom went along – it was usually just Sam and Mr Beaver. They would motor to the border and cross into Canada. There Mr Beaver would hire a bush pilot to fly them to the lake where his camp was, for a few days of fishing and loafing and exploring. Mr Beaver did most of the fishing and loafing. Sam did the exploring. And then the pilot would return to take them out. His name was Shorty. They would hear the sound of his motor and run out and wave and watch him glide down on to the lake and taxi his plane in to the dock. These were the pleasantest days of Sam's life, these days in the woods, far, far from everywhere – no automobiles, no roads, no people, no noise, no school, no homework, no problems, except the problem of getting lost. And, of course, the problem of what to be when he grew up. Every boy has *that* problem.

After supper that evening, Sam and his father sat for a while on the porch. Sam was reading a bird book.

'Pop,' said Sam, 'do you think we'll be coming back to camp again about a month from now – I mean, in about thirty-five days or something like that?'

'I guess so,' replied Mr Beaver. 'I certainly hope so. But why thirty-five days? What's so special about thirty-five days?'

'Oh, nothing,' said Sam. 'I just thought it might be very nice around here in thirty-five days.'

'That's the craziest thing I ever heard of,' said Mr Beaver. 'It's nice here *all* the time.'

Sam went indoors. He knew a lot about

birds, and he knew it would take a swan about thirty-five days to hatch her eggs. He hoped he could be at the pond to see the young ones when they came out of the eggs.

Sam kept a diary – a daybook about his life. It was just a cheap notebook that was always by his bed. Every night, before he turned in, he would write in the book. He wrote about things he had done, things he had seen, and thoughts he had had. Sometimes he drew a picture. He always ended by asking himself a question so he would have something to think about while falling asleep. On the day he found the swan's nest, this is what Sam wrote in his diary:

I saw a pair of trumpeter swans today on a small pond east of camp. The female has a nest with eggs in it. I saw three, but I'm going to put four in the picture – I think she was laying another one. This is the greatest discovery I ever made in my entire life. I did

not tell Pop. My bird book says baby swans are called cygnets. I am going back tomorrow to visit the great swans again. I heard a fox bark today. Why does a fox bark? Is it because he is mad, or worried, or hungry, or because he is sending a message to another fox? *Why does a fox bark?*

Sam closed his notebook, undressed, crawled into his bunk, and lay there with his eyes closed, wondering why a fox barks. In a few minutes he was asleep.

2. The Pond

THE POND Sam had discovered on that spring morning was seldom visited by any human being. All winter, snow had covered the ice; the pond lay cold and still under its white blanket. Most of the time there wasn't a sound to be heard. The frog was asleep. The chipmunk was asleep. Occasionally a jay would cry out. And sometimes at night the fox would bark – a high, rasping bark. Winter seemed to last forever.

But one day a change came over the woods and the pond. Warm air, soft and kind, blew through the trees. The ice, which had softened during the night, began to melt. Patches of open water appeared. All the creatures that lived in the pond and in the woods were glad to feel the warmth. They heard and felt the breath of spring, and they stirred with new life and hope. There was a good, new smell in the air, a smell of earth waking after its long sleep. The frog, buried in the mud at the bottom of the pond, knew that spring was here. The chickadee knew and was delighted (almost everything delights a chickadee). The vixen, dozing in her den, knew she would soon have cubs. Every creature knew that a better, easier time was at hand – warmer days, pleasanter nights. Trees were putting out green buds; the buds were swelling. Birds began arriving from the south. A pair of ducks flew in. The red-winged blackbird arrived and scouted the pond for nesting sites. A small sparrow with a white throat arrived and sang, 'Oh, sweet Canada, Canada, Canada!'

And if you had been sitting by the pond on that first warm day of spring, suddenly, toward the end of the afternoon, you would have heard a stirring sound high above you in the air – a sound like the sound of trumpets.

'Ko-hoh, ko-hoh!'

And if you had looked up, you would have seen, high overhead, two great white birds. They flew swiftly, their legs stretched out straight behind, their long white necks stretched out ahead, their powerful wings beating steady and strong. 'Ko-hoh, ko-hoh, ko-hoh!' A thrilling noise in the sky, the trumpeting of swans.

When the birds spotted the pond, they began circling, looking the place over from the air. Then they glided down and came to rest in the water, folding their long wings neatly along their sides and turning their heads this way and that to study their new surroundings. They were Trumpeter Swans, pure white birds with black bills. They had

liked the looks of the swampy pond and had decided to make it their home for a while and raise a family.

The two swans were tired from the long flight. They were glad to be down out of the sky. They paddled slowly about and then began feeding, thrusting their necks into the shallow water and pulling roots and plants from the bottom. Everything about the swans was white except their bills and their feet; these were black. They carried their heads high. The pond seemed a different place because of their arrival.

For the next few days, the swans rested. When they were hungry, they ate. When they were thirsty – which was a great deal of the time – they drank. On the tenth day, the female began looking around to find a place to build her nest.

In the spring of the year, nest-building is uppermost in a bird's mind: it is the most important thing there is. If she picks a good place, she stands a good chance of hatching her eggs and rearing her young. If she picks a poor place, she may fail to raise a family. The female swan knew this; she knew the decision she was making was extremely important.

The two swans first investigated the upper end of the pond, where a stream flowed slowly in. It was pleasant there, with reeds and bulrushes. Red-winged Blackbirds were busy nesting in this part of the pond, and a pair of Mallard Ducks were courting. Then the swans swam to the lower end of the pond, a marsh with woods on one side and a deer meadow on the other. It was lonely here. From one shore, a point of land extended out into the pond. It was a sandy strip, like a little peninsula. And at the tip of it, a few feet out into the water, was a tiny island, hardly bigger than a dining table. One small tree grew on the island, and there were rocks and ferns and grasses.

'Take a look at this!' exclaimed the female, as she swam round and around.

'Ko-hoh!' replied her husband, who liked to have someone ask his advice.

The swan stepped cautiously out on to the island. The spot seemed made to order – just right for a nesting place. While the male swan floated close by, watching, she snooped about until she found a pleasant spot on the ground. She sat down, to see how it felt to be sitting there. She decided it was the right size for her body. It was nicely located, a couple of feet from the water's edge. Very convenient. She turned to her husband.

'What do you think?' she said.

'An ideal location!' he replied. 'A perfect place! And I will tell you *why* it's a perfect place,' he continued, majestically. 'If an enemy – a fox or a coon or a coyote or a skunk – wanted to reach this spot with murder in his heart, he'd have to enter the water and get wet. And before he could enter the water, he'd have to walk the whole length of that point of land. And by that time we'd see him or hear him, and I would give him a hard time.'

The male stretched out his great wings, eight feet from tip to tip, and gave the water a mighty clout to show his strength. This made him feel better right away. When a Trumpeter Swan hits an enemy with his wing, it is like being hit by a baseball bat. A male swan, by the way, is called a 'cob'. No one knows why, but that's what he's called. A good many animals have special names: a male goose is called a gander, a male cow is called a bull, a male sheep is called a ram, a male chicken is called a rooster, and so on. Anyway, the thing to remember is that a male swan is called a cob.

The cob's wife pretended not to notice that her husband was showing off, but she saw it, all right, and she was proud of his strength and his courage. As husbands go, he was a good one.

The cob watched his beautiful wife sitting

there on the tiny island. To his great joy, he saw her begin to turn slowly round and around, keeping always in the same spot, treading the mud and grass. She was making the first motions of nesting. First she squatted down in the place she had chosen. Then she twisted round and around, tamping the earth with her broad webbed feet, hollowing it out to make it like a saucer. Then she reached out and pulled twigs and grasses toward her and dropped them at her sides and under her tail, shaping the nest to her body.

The cob floated close to his mate. He studied every move she made.

'Now another medium-sized stick, my love,' he said. And she poked her splendid long white graceful neck as far as it would go, picked up a stick, and placed it at her side.

'Now another bit of coarse grass,' said the cob, with great dignity.

The female reached for grasses, for moss, for twigs – anything that was handy. Slowly, carefully, she built up the nest until she was sitting on a big grassy mound. She worked at the task for a couple of hours, then knocked off for the day and slid into the pond again, to take a drink and have lunch.

'A fine start!' said the cob, as he gazed back at the nest. 'A perfect beginning! I don't know how you manage it so cleverly.'

'It comes naturally,' replied his wife. 'There's a lot of work to it, but on the whole it is pleasant work.'

'Yes,' said the cob. 'And when you're done, you have something to show for your trouble – you have a swan's nest, six feet across. What other bird can say that?'

'Well,' said his wife, 'maybe an eagle can say it.'

'Yes, but in that case it wouldn't be a swan's nest, it would be an eagle's nest, and it would be high up in some old dead tree somewhere, instead of right down near the water, with all the conveniences that go with water.'

They both laughed at this. Then they began trumpeting and splashing and scooping up water and throwing it on their backs, darting about as though they had suddenly gone crazy with delight.

'Ko-hoh! Ko-hoh! Ko-hoh!' they cried.

Every wild creature within a mile and a half of the pond heard the trumpeting of the swans. The fox heard, the raccoon heard, the skunk heard. One pair of ears heard that did not belong to a wild creature. But the swans did not know that.

3. A Visitor

ONE DAY, almost a week later, the swan slipped quietly into her nest and laid an egg. Each day she tried to deposit one egg in the nest. Sometimes she succeeded, sometimes she didn't. There were now three eggs, and she was ready to lay a fourth.

As she sat there, with her husband, the cob, floating gracefully nearby, she had a strange feeling that she was being watched. It made her uneasy. Birds don't like to be stared at. They particularly dislike being stared at when they are on a nest. So the swan twisted and turned and peered everywhere. She gazed intently at the point of land that jutted out into the pond near the nest. With her sharp eyes, she searched the nearby shore for signs of an intruder. What she finally saw gave her the surprise of her life. There, seated on a log on the point of land, was a small boy. He was being very quiet, and he had no gun.

'Do you see what I see?' the swan whispered to her husband.

'No. What?'

'Over there. On that log. It's a boy! *Now* what are we going to do?'

'How did a boy get here?' whispered the cob. 'We are deep in the wilds of Canada. There are no human beings for miles around.'

'That's what I thought too,' she replied. 'But if that isn't a boy over there on that log, my name isn't Cygnus Buccinator.'

The cob was furious. 'I didn't fly all the way north into Canada to get involved with a *boy*,' he said. 'We came here to this idyllic spot, this remote little hideaway, so we could enjoy some well-deserved privacy.'

'Well,' said his wife, 'I'm sorry to see the boy, too, but I must say he's behaving himself. He sees us, but he's not throwing stones. He's not throwing sticks. He's not messing around. He's simply observing.'

'I do not *wish* to be observed,' complained the cob. 'I did not travel all this immense distance into the heart of Canada to be observed. Furthermore, I don't want *you* to be observed – except by me. You're laying an egg – that is, I *hope* you are – and you are entitled to privacy. It has been my experience that all boys throw stones and sticks – it is their nature. I'm going over and strike that boy with my powerful wing, and he'll think he has been hit with a billy club. I'll knock him cold!'

'Now, just wait a minute!' said the swan. 'There's no use starting a fight. This boy is not bothering me at the moment. He's not bothering you either.'

'But how did he *get* here?' said the cob, who was no longer talking in a whisper but was beginning to shout. 'How did he get here? Boys can't fly, and there are no roads in this part of Canada. We're fifty miles from the nearest highway.'

'Maybe he's lost,' said the swan. 'Maybe he's starving to death. Maybe he wants to rob the nest and eat the eggs, but I doubt it. He doesn't look hungry. Anyway, I've started this nest, and I have three beautiful eggs, and the boy's behaving himself at the moment, and I intend to go right ahead and try for a fourth egg.'

'Good luck, my love!' said the cob. 'I shall be here at your side to defend you if anything happens. Lay the egg!'

For the next hour, the cob paddled slowly round and around the tiny island, keeping watch. His wife remained quietly on the nest. Sam sat on his log, hardly moving a muscle. He was spellbound at the sight of the swans. They were the biggest water birds he had ever seen. He had heard their trumpeting and had searched the woods and swamps until he had found the pond and located the nest. Sam knew enough about birds to know that these were Trumpeters. Sam always felt happy when he was in a wild place among wild creatures. Sitting on his log, watching the swans, he had the same good feeling some people get when they are sitting in church.

After he had watched for an hour, Sam got up. He walked slowly and quietly away, putting one foot straight ahead of the other, Indian-fashion, hardly making a sound. The swans watched him go. When the female left the nest, she turned and looked back. There, lying safely in the soft feathers at the bottom of the nest, was the fourth egg. The cob waddled out on to the island and looked in the nest.

'A masterpiece!' he said. 'An egg of supreme

beauty and perfect proportions. I would say that that egg is almost five inches in length.'

His wife was pleased.

When the swan had laid five eggs, she felt satisfied. She gazed at them proudly. Then she settled herself on the nest to keep her eggs warm. Carefully, she reached down with her bill and poked each egg until it was in just the right spot to receive the heat from her body. The cob cruised around close by, to keep her company and protect her from enemies. He knew that a fox prowled somewhere in the woods; he had heard him barking on nights when the hunting was good.

Days passed, and still the swan sat quietly on the five eggs. Nights passed. She sat and sat, giving her warmth to the eggs. No one disturbed her. The boy was gone – perhaps he would never come back. Inside of each egg, something was happening that she couldn't see: a little swan was taking shape. As the weeks went by, the days grew longer, the nights grew shorter. When a rainy day came, the swan just sat still and let it rain.

'My dear,' said her husband, the cob, one afternoon, 'do you never find your duties onerous or irksome? Do you never tire of sitting in one place and in one position, covering the eggs, with no diversions, no pleasures, no escapades, or capers? Do you never suffer from boredom?'

'No,' replied his wife. 'Not really.'

'Isn't it uncomfortable to sit on eggs?'

'Yes, it is,' replied the wife. 'But I can put up with a certain amount of discomfort for the sake of bringing young swans into the world.'

'Do you know how many more days you must sit?' he asked.

'Haven't any idea,' she said. 'But I notice that the ducks at the other end of the pond have hatched their young ones; I notice that the Red-winged Blackbirds have hatched theirs, and the other evening I saw a Striped Skunk hunting along the shore, and she had four little skunks with her. So I think I must be getting near the end of my time. With any luck, we will soon be able to see our children – our beautiful little cygnets.'

'Don't you ever feel the pangs of hunger or suffer the tortures of thirst?' asked the cob.

'Yes, I do,' said his mate. 'As a matter of fact, I could use a drink right now.'

The afternoon was warm; the sun was bright. The swan decided she could safely leave her eggs for a few minutes. She stood up. First she pushed some loose feathers around the eggs, hiding them from view and giving them a warm covering in her absence. Then she stepped off the nest and entered the water. She took several quick drinks. Then she glided over to a shallow place, thrust her head under water, and pulled up tender greens from the bottom. She next took a bath by tossing water over herself. Then she waddled out on

to a grassy bank and stood there, preening her feathers.

The swan felt good. She had no idea that an enemy was near. She failed to notice the Red Fox as he watched her from his hiding place behind a clump of bushes. The fox had been attracted to the pond by the sound of splashing water. He hoped he would find a goose. Now he sniffed the air and smelled the

swan. Her back was turned, so he began creeping slowly toward her. She would be too big for him to carry, but he decided he would kill her anyway and get a taste of blood. The cob, her husband, was still floating on the pond. He spied the fox first.

'Look out!' he trumpeted. 'Look out for the fox, who is creeping toward you even as I speak, his eyes bright, his bushy tail out straight, his mind lusting for blood, his belly almost touching the ground! You are in grave danger, and we must act immediately.'

While the cob was making this elegant speech of warning, something happened that surprised everybody. Just as the fox was about to spring and sink his teeth in the swan's neck, a stick came hurtling through the air. It struck the fox full on the nose, and he turned and ran away. The two swans couldn't imagine what had happened. Then they noticed a movement in the bushes. Out stepped Sam Beaver, the boy who had visited them a month ago. Sam was grinning. In his hand he held another stick, in case the fox should return. But the fox was in no mood to return. He had a very sore nose, and he had lost his appetite for fresh swan.

'Hello,' said Sam in a low voice.

'Ko-hoh, ko-hoh!' replied the cob.

'Ko-hoh!' said his wife. The pond rang with the trumpet sounds – sounds of triumph over the fox, sounds of victory and gladness.

Sam was thrilled at the noise of swans, which some people say is like the sound of a French horn. He walked slowly around the shore to the little point of land near the island

and sat down on his log. The swans now realized, beyond any doubt, that the boy was their friend. He had saved the swan's life. He had been in the right place at the right time and with the right ammunition. The swans felt grateful. The cob swam over toward Sam, climbed out of the pond, and stood close to the boy, looking at him in a friendly way and arching his neck gracefully. Once, he ran his neck far out, cautiously, and almost touched the boy. Sam never moved a muscle. His heart thumped from excitement and joy.

The female paddled back to her nest and returned to the job of warming the eggs. She felt lucky to be alive.

That night before Sam crawled into his bunk at camp, he got out his notebook and found a pencil. This is what he wrote:

I don't know of anything in the entire world more wonderful to look at than a nest with eggs in it. An egg, because it contains life, is the most perfect thing there is. It is beautiful and mysterious. An egg is a far finer thing than a tennis ball or a cake of soap. A tennis ball will always be just a tennis ball. A cake of soap will always be just a cake of soap – until it gets so small nobody wants it and they throw it away. But an egg will some day be a living creature. A swan's egg will open and out will come a little swan. A nest is almost as wonderful and mysterious as an egg. How does a bird know how to make a nest? Nobody ever taught her. How does a bird know how to build a nest?

Sam closed his notebook, said goodnight to his father, blew out his lamp, and climbed into his bunk. He lay there wondering how a bird knows how to build a nest. Pretty soon his eyes closed, and he was asleep.

4. The Cygnets

DURING the night, the swan thought she heard a pipping sound from the eggs. And in the hour just before dawn, she was sure she felt a slight movement under her breast, as though a tiny body were wiggling there. Perhaps the eggs at last were hatching. Eggs, of course, can't wiggle, so the swan decided she must have something under her that wasn't an egg. She sat perfectly still, listening and waiting. The cob floated nearby, keeping watch.

A little swan enclosed in an egg has a

hard time getting out. It never *would* get out if Nature had not provided it with two important things: a powerful neck-muscle and a small dagger-tooth on the tip of its bill. This tooth is sharp, and the baby swan uses it to pick a hole in the tough shell of the egg. Once the hole is made, the rest is easy. The cygnet can breathe now; it just keeps wiggling until it wiggles free.

The cob was expecting to become a father any minute now. The idea of fatherhood made him feel poetical and proud. He began to talk to his wife.

'Here I glide, swanlike,' he said, 'while earth is bathed in wonder and beauty. Now, slowly, the light of day comes into our sky. A mist hangs low over the pond. The mist rises slowly, like steam from a kettle, while I glide, swanlike, while eggs hatch, while young swans come into existence. I glide and glide. The light strengthens. The air becomes warmer. Gradually the mist disappears. I glide, I glide, swanlike. Birds sing their early song. Frogs that have croaked in the night stop croaking and are silent. Still I glide, ceaselessly, like a swan.'

'Of course you glide like a swan,' said his wife. 'How else could you glide? You couldn't glide like a moose, could you?'

'Well, no. That is quite true. Thank you, my dear, for correcting me.' The cob felt taken aback by his mate's commonsense remark. He enjoyed speaking in fancy phrases and graceful language, and he liked to think of himself as gliding swanlike. He decided he'd better do more gliding and less talking.

All morning long, the swan heard the pipping of the shells. And every once in a while, she felt something wriggle beneath her in the nest. It was an odd sensation. The eggs had been quiet for so many, many days – thirty-five days in all – and now at last they were stirring with life. She knew that the proper thing to do was to sit still.

Late in the afternoon, the swan was

rewarded for her patience. She gazed down, and there, pushing her feathers aside, came a tiny head – the first baby, the first cygnet. It was soft and downy. Unlike its parents, it was grey. Its feet and legs were the colour of mustard. Its eyes were bright. On unsteady legs, it pushed its way up until it stood beside its mother, looking around at the world it was seeing for the first time. Its mother spoke softly to it, and it was glad to hear her voice. It was glad to breathe the air, after being cooped up so long inside an egg.

The cob, who had been watching intently all day, saw the little head appear. His heart leapt up with joy. 'A cygnet!' he cried. 'A cygnet at last! I am a father, with all the pleasant duties and awesome responsibilities of fatherhood. O blessed little son of mine, how good it is to see your face peering through the protecting feathers of your mother's breast, under these fair skies, with the pond so quiet and peaceful in the long light of afternoon!'

'What makes you think it's a son?' inquired his wife. 'For all you know, it's a daughter. Anyway, it's a cygnet, and it's alive and healthy. I can feel others under me, too. Perhaps we'll get a good hatch. We may even get all five. We'll know by tomorrow.'

'I have every confidence that we will,' said the cob.

Next morning very early, Sam Beaver crawled out of his bunk while his father was still asleep. Sam dressed and lit a fire in the stove. He fried a few strips of bacon, toasted two slices of bread, poured a glass of milk, and sat down and ate breakfast. When he was through, he found a pencil and paper and wrote a note.

I have gone for a walk. Will be back for lunch.

Sam left the note where his father would find it; then he took his field glasses and his compass, fastened his hunting knife to his belt, and set out through the woods and over the swamp to the pond where the swans lived.

He approached the pond cautiously, his field glasses slung over his shoulder. It was still only a little after seven o'clock; the sun was pale, the air was chill. The morning smelled delicious. When he reached his log, Sam sat down and adjusted his glasses. Seen through the glasses, the nesting swan appeared to be only a few feet away. She was sitting very close, not moving. The cob was nearby. Both birds were listening and waiting. Both birds saw Sam, but they didn't mind his being there – in fact, they rather liked it. They *were* surprised at the field glasses, though.

'The boy seems to have very big eyes today,' whispered the cob. 'His eyes are enormous.'

'I think those big eyes are actually a pair of field glasses,' replied the swan. 'I'm not sure, but I think that when a person looks through field glasses, everything appears closer and bigger.'

'Will the boy's glasses make me appear even larger than I am?' asked the cob, hopefully.

'I think so,' said the swan.

'Oh, well, I *like* that,' said the cob. 'I like that very much. Perhaps the boy's glasses will make me appear not only larger than I am but even more graceful than I am. Do you think so?'

'It's possible,' said his wife, 'but it's not likely. You'd better not get *too* graceful – it might go to your head. You're quite a vain bird.'

'All swans are vain,' said the cob. 'It is right for swans to feel proud, graceful – that's what swans are for.'

Sam could not make out what the swans were saying; he merely knew they were having a conversation, and just hearing them talk stirred his blood. It satisfied him to be keeping company with these two great birds in the wilderness. He was perfectly happy.

In midmorning, when the sun had gained the sky, Sam lifted his glasses again and focused them on the nest. At last he saw what he had come to see: a tiny head, thrusting through the mother's feathers, the head of a baby Trumpeter. The youngster scrambled up on to the edge of the nest. Sam could see its grey head and neck, its body covered with soft down, its yellow legs and feet with their webs for swimming. Soon another cygnet appeared. Then another. Then the first one worked his way down into his mother's feathers again, for warmth. Then one tried to climb up his mother's back, but her feathers were slippery, and he slid off and settled himself neatly at her side. The swan just sat and sat, enjoying her babies, watching them gain the use of their legs.

An hour went by. One of the cygnets, more daring than the others, left the nest and teetered around on the shore of the little island. When this happened, the mother swan stood up. She decided the time had come to lead her children into the water.

'Come on!' she said. 'And stay together! Note carefully what I do. Then you do the same. Swimming is easy.'

'One, two, three, four, five,' Sam counted. 'One, two, three, four, five. Five cygnets, just as sure as I'm alive!'

The cob, as he saw his children approach the water, felt that he should act like a father. He began by making a speech.

'Welcome to the pond and the swamp adjacent!' he said. 'Welcome to the world that contains this lonely pond, this splendid marsh, unspoiled and wild! Welcome to sunlight and shadow, wind and weather; welcome to water! The water is a swan's particular element, as you will soon discover. Swimming is no problem for a swan. Welcome to danger, which you must guard against – the vile fox with his stealthy tread and sharp teeth, the offensive otter who swims up under you and tries to grab you by the leg, the stinking skunk who hunts by night and blends with the shadows, the coyote who hunts and howls and is bigger than a fox. Beware of lead pellets that lie on the bottom of all ponds, left there by the guns of hunters. Don't eat them – they'll poison you! Be vigilant, be strong, be brave, be graceful, and *always* follow me! I will go first, then you will come along in single file, and your devoted mother will bring up the rear. Enter the water quietly and confidently!'

The mother swan, glad the speech was over, stepped into the water and called her little ones. The cygnets gazed for a second at the water, then tottered forward, gave a jump, and were afloat. The water felt good. Swimming was simple – nothing to it. The water was good to drink. Each baby dipped up a mouthful. Their happy father arched his long graceful neck over and around them, protectively. Then he set off very slowly, with the cygnets following along in single file. Their mother brought up the rear.

'What a sight!' Sam said to himself. 'What

a terrific sight! Seven Trumpeters all in line, five of them just out of the egg. This is my lucky day.' He hardly noticed how stiff he had become from sitting so long on the log.

Like all fathers, the cob wanted to show off his children to somebody. So he led the cygnets to where Sam was. They all stepped out of the water and stood in front of the boy – all but the mother swan. She stayed behind.

'Ko-hoh!' said the cob.

'Hello!' said Sam, who hadn't expected anything like this and hardly dared breathe.

The first cygnet looked at Sam and said, 'Beep.' The second cygnet looked at Sam and said, 'Beep.' The third cygnet greeted Sam the same way. So did the fourth. The fifth cygnet was different. He opened his mouth but didn't say a thing. He made an effort to say beep, but no sound came. So instead, he stuck his little neck out, took hold of one of Sam's shoelaces, and gave it a pull. He tugged at the lace for a moment. It came untied. Then he let it go. It was like a greeting. Sam grinned.

The cob now looked worried. He ran his long white neck between the cygnets and the boy and guided the babies back to the water and to their mother.

'Follow me!' said the cob. And he led them off, full of grace and bursting with pride.

When the mother thought her young ones had had enough swimming and might be chilly, she stepped out on to a sandy shore and squatted down and called them. They quickly followed her out of the pond and burrowed down under her feathers to get warm. In a moment there wasn't a cygnet in sight.

At noon, Sam got up and walked back to camp, his mind full of what he had seen. Next day, he and his father heard Shorty's motor in the sky and saw the plane approaching. They grabbed their duffel bags. 'Goodbye, camp! See you in the fall!' said Mr Beaver, as he shut the door and gave it a pat. He and Sam

climbed into the plane and were soon aloft, on their way home to Montana. Mr Beaver did not know that his son had seen a Trumpeter Swan bring off her young ones. Sam kept the matter to himself.

'If I live to be a hundred years old,' thought Sam, 'I'll never forget what it feels like to have my shoelace pulled by a baby swan.'

Sam and his father were late arriving home at the ranch, but late as it was, Sam got out his diary before he turned in for the night. He wrote:

There are five cygnets. They are sort of a dirty brownish-grey colour, but very cute. Their legs are yellow, like mustard. The old cob led them right up to me. I wasn't expecting this, but I kept very still. Four of the babies said beep. The fifth one tried to, but he couldn't. He took hold of my shoelace as though it was a worm and gave it a tug and untied it. I wonder what I'm going to be when I grow up?

He switched off the light, pulled the sheet up over his head, and fell asleep wondering what he was going to be when he grew up.

5. Louis

ONE EVENING a few weeks later, when the cygnets were asleep, the swan said to the cob, 'Have you noticed anything different about one of our children, the one we call Louis?'

'Different?' replied the cob. 'In what way is Louis different from his brothers and sisters? Louis looks all right to me. He is growing well; he swims and dives beautifully. He eats well. He will soon have his flight feathers.'

'Oh, he *looks* all right,' said the swan. 'And heaven knows he eats enough. He's healthy and bright and a great swimmer. But have you ever heard Louis make any sound, as the others do? Have you ever heard him use his voice or say anything? Have you ever heard him utter a single beep or a single burble?'

'Come to think of it, I never have,' replied the cob, who was beginning to look worried.

'Have you ever heard Louis say goodnight to us, as the others do? Have you ever heard him say good morning, as the others do in their charming little way, burbling and beeping?'

'Now that you mention it, I never have,' said the cob. 'Goodness! What are you getting at? Do you wish me to believe that I have a son who is *defective* in any way? Such a revelation would distress me greatly. I want everything to go smoothly in my family life so that I can glide gracefully and serenely, now in the prime of my life, without being haunted by worry or disappointment. Fatherhood is quite a burden, at best. I do not want the added strain of having a defective child, a child that has something the matter with him.'

'Well,' said the wife, 'I've been watching Louis lately. It is my opinion the little fellow can't talk. I've never heard him make one sound. I think he came into the world lacking a voice. If he had a voice, he'd use it, same as the others do.'

'Why, this is terrible!' said the cob. 'This is distressing beyond words. This is a very serious matter.'

His wife looked at him in amusement. 'It's not too serious now,' she said. 'But it *will* be serious two or three years from now when Louis falls in love, as he will surely do. A young male swan will be greatly handicapped in finding a mate if he is unable to say ko-hoh, ko-hoh, or if he can't utter the usual endearments to the young female of his choice.'

'Are you sure?' asked the cob.

'Certainly I'm sure,' she replied. 'I can

remember perfectly well the springtime, years ago, when you fell in love with me and began chasing after me. What a sight you were, and what a lot of noise you made! It was in Montana, remember?'

'Of course I remember,' said the cob.

'Well, the thing that attracted me most to you was your voice – your wonderful voice.'

'It *was*?' said the cob.

'Yes. You had the finest, most powerful, most resonant voice of any of the young male swans in the Red Rock Lakes National Wildlife Refuge in Montana.'

'I *did*?' said the cob.

'Yes, indeed. Every time I heard you say something in that deep voice of yours, I was ready to go anywhere with you.'

'You *were*?' said the cob. He was obviously delighted with his wife's praise. It tickled his vanity and made him feel great. He had always fancied himself as having a fine voice, and now to hear it from his wife's own lips was a real thrill. In the pleasure of the moment, he forgot all about Louis and thought entirely of himself. And, of course, he did remember that enchanted springtime on the lake in Montana when he had fallen in love. He remembered how pretty the swan had been, how young and innocent she seemed, how attractive, how desirable. Now he realized fully that he would never have been able to woo her and win her if he had been unable to *say* anything.

'We'll not worry about Louis for the time being,' said the swan. 'He's still very young. But we must watch him next winter when we are in Montana for the season. We must stay together as a family until we see how Louis makes out.'

She walked over to where her sleeping cygnets were and settled down next to them. The night was chill. Carefully, she lifted one wing and covered the cygnets with it. They stirred in their sleep and drew close to her.

The cob stood quietly, thinking about what his wife had just told him. He was a brave, noble bird, and already he was beginning to work out a plan for his little son Louis.

'If it's really true that Louis has no voice,' said the cob to himself, 'then I shall provide him with a device of some sort, to enable him to make a lot of noise. There must be *some* way out of this difficulty. After all, my son is a Trumpeter Swan; he should have a voice like a trumpet. But first I will test him to make certain that what his mother says is true.'

The cob was unable to sleep that night. He stood on one leg, quietly, but sleep never came. Next morning, after everyone had enjoyed a good breakfast, he led Louis apart from the others.

'Louis,' he said, 'I wish to speak to you alone. Let's just you and I take a swim by ourselves to the other end of the pond, where we can talk privately without being interrupted.'

Louis was surprised by this. But he nodded

his head and followed his father, swimming strongly in his wake. He did not understand why his father wanted to speak to him alone, without his brothers and sisters.

'Now!' said the cob, when they reached the upper end of the pond. 'Here we are, gracefully floating, supremely buoyant, at some distance from the others, in perfect surroundings – a fine morning, with the pond quiet except for the song of the blackbirds, making the air sweet.'

'I wish my father would get to the point,' thought Louis.

'This is an ideal place for our conference,' continued the cob. 'There is something I feel I should discuss with you very candidly and openly – something that concerns your future. We need not range over the whole spectrum of bird life but just confine our talk to the one essential thing that is before us on this unusual occasion.'

'Oh, I *wish* my father would get to the

point,' thought Louis, who by this time was getting very nervous.

'It has come to my attention, Louis,' continued the cob, 'that you rarely *say* anything. In fact, I can't recall ever hearing you utter a sound. I have never heard you speak, or say ko-hoh, or cry out, either in fear or in joy. This is most unusual for a young Trumpeter. It is serious. Louis, let me hear you say beep. Go ahead, say it! Say beep!'

Poor Louis! While his father watched, he took a deep breath, opened his mouth, and let the air out, hoping it would say beep. But there wasn't a sound.

'Try again, Louis!' said his father. 'Perhaps you're not making enough of an effort.'

Louis tried again. It was no use. No sound came from his throat. He shook his head, sadly.

'Watch me!' said the cob. He raised his neck to its full height and cried ko-hoh so loud it was heard by every creature for miles around.

'Now let me hear you go beep!' he commanded. 'Say beep, Louis – loud and clear!'

Louis tried. He couldn't beep.

'Let me hear you burble! Go ahead and burble! Like this: burble, burble, burble.'

Louis tried to burble. He couldn't do it. No sound came.

'Well,' said the cob, 'I guess it's no use. I guess you are dumb.'

When he heard the word 'dumb,' Louis felt like crying. The cob saw that he had hurt Louis's feelings.

'You misunderstand me, my son,' he said in a comforting voice. 'You failed to understand my use of the word "dumb", which has two meanings. If I had called you a dumb cluck or a dumb bunny, that would have meant that I had a poor opinion of your intelligence. Actually, I think you are perhaps the brightest, smartest, most intelligent of all my cygnets.

Words sometimes have two meanings; the word 'dumb' is such a word. A person who can't see is called blind. A person who can't hear is called deaf. A person who can't speak is called dumb. That simply means he can't say anything. Do you understand?'

Louis nodded his head. He felt better, and he was grateful to his father for explaining that the word had two meanings. He still felt awfully unhappy, though.

'Do not let an unnatural sadness settle over you, Louis,' said the cob. 'Swans must be cheerful, not sad; graceful, not awkward; brave, not cowardly. Remember that the world is full of youngsters who have some sort of handicap that they must overcome. *You* apparently have a speech defect. I am sure you will overcome it, in time. There may even be some slight advantage, at your age, in not being able to say anything. It compels you to be a good listener. The world is full of talkers, but it is rare to find anyone who listens. And I assure you that you can pick up more information when you are listening than when you are talking.'

'My father does quite a lot of talking himself,' thought Louis.

'Some people,' continued the cob, 'go through life chattering and making a lot of noise with their mouth; they never really *listen*

57

to anything – they are too busy expressing their opinions, which are often unsound or based on bad information. Therefore, my son, be of good cheer! Enjoy life; learn to fly! Eat well; drink well! Use your ears; use your eyes! And I promise that some day I will make it possible for you to use your voice. There are mechanical devices that convert air into beautiful sounds. One such device is called a trumpet. I saw a trumpet once, in my travels. I think you may need a trumpet in order to live a full life. I've never *known* a Trumpeter Swan to need a trumpet, but your case is different. I intend to get you what you need. I don't know how I will manage this, but in the fullness of time it shall be accomplished. And now that our talk has come to a close, let us return gracefully to the other end of the pond, where your mother and your brothers and sisters await us!'

The cob turned and swam off. Louis followed. It had been an unhappy morning for him. He felt frightened at being different from his brothers and sisters. It scared him to be different. He couldn't understand why he had come into the world without a voice. Everyone else seemed to have a voice. Why didn't he? 'Fate is cruel,' he thought. 'Fate is cruel to me.' Then he remembered that his father had promised to help, and he felt better. Soon they joined the others, and everyone started water games, and Louis joined in, dipping and splashing and diving and twisting. Louis could splash water farther than any of the others, but he couldn't shout while he was doing it. To be able to shout while you are splashing water is half the fun.

6. Off to Montana

A T THE end of the summer, the cob
gathered his family around him and
made an announcement. 'Children,' he began,
'I have news for you. Summer is drawing to a
close. Leaves are turning red, pink, and pale
yellow. Soon the leaves will fall. The time has
come for us to leave this pond. The time has
come for us to go.'

'Go?' cried all the cygnets except Louis.

'Certainly,' replied their father. 'You children
are old enough to learn the facts of life, and
the principal fact of our life right now is this:

we can't stay in this marvellous location much longer.'

'Why not?' cried all the cygnets except Louis.

'Because summer is over,' said the cob, 'and it is the way of swans to leave their nesting site at summer's end and travel south to a milder place where the food supply is good. I know that you are all fond of this pretty pond, this marvellous marsh, these reedy shores and restful retreats. You have found life pleasant and amusing here. You have learned to dive and swim under water. You have enjoyed our daily recreational trips when we formed in line, myself in front swimming gracefully, like a locomotive, and your charming mother bringing up the rear, like a caboose. Day-long, you have listened and learned. You have avoided the odious otter and the cruel coyote. You have listened to the little owl that says co-co-co-co. You have heard the partridge say kwit-kwit. At night you have dropped off to sleep to the sound of frogs – the voices of the night. But these pleasures and pastimes, these adventures, these games and frolics, these beloved sights and sounds must come to an end. All things come to an end. It is time for us to go.'

'Where will we go?' cried all the cygnets except Louis. 'Where will we go, ko-hoh, ko-hoh? Where will we go, ko-hoh, ko-hoh?'

'We will fly south to Montana,' replied the cob.

'What is Montana?' asked all the cygnets except Louis. 'What is Montana – banana, banana? What is Montana – banana, banana?'

'Montana,' said their father, 'is a state of the Union. And there, in a lovely valley surrounded by high mountains, are the Red Rock Lakes, which nature has designed especially for swans. In these lakes you will enjoy warm water, arising from hidden springs. Here, ice never forms, no matter how cold the nights. In the Red Rock Lakes, you will find other Trumpeter

Swans, as well as the lesser waterfowl – the geese and the ducks. There are few enemies. No gunners. Plenty of muskrat houses. Free grain. Games every day. What more can a swan ask, in the long, long cold of winter?'

Louis listened to all this in amazement. He wanted to ask his father how they would learn to fly and how they would find Montana even after they learned to fly. He began to worry about getting lost. But he wasn't able to ask any questions. He just had to listen.

One of his brothers spoke up.

'Father,' he said, 'you said we would *fly* south. I don't know *how* to fly. I've never been up in the air.'

'True,' replied the cob. 'But flying is largely a matter of having the right attitude – plus, of course, good wing feathers. Flying consists of three parts. First, the take-off, during which there is a lot of fuss and commotion, a lot of splashing and rapid beating of the wings.

Second, the ascent, or gaining of altitude – this requires hard work and fast wing action. Third, the levelling-off, the steady elevated flight, high in air, wings beating slower now, beating strongly and regularly, carrying us swiftly and surely from zone to zone as we cry ko-hoh, ko-hoh, with all the earth stretched out far below.'

'It sounds very nice,' said the cygnet, 'but I'm not sure I can do it. I might get dizzy way up there – if I look down.'

'Don't *look* down!' said his father. 'Look straight ahead. And don't lose your nerve. Besides, swans do not get dizzy – they feel wonderful in the air. They feel exalted.'

'What does "exalted" mean?' asked the cygnet.

'It means you will feel strong, glad, firm, high, proud, successful, satisfied, powerful, and elevated – as though you had conquered life and had a high purpose.'

Louis listened to all this with great

attention. The idea of flying frightened him. 'I won't be able to say ko-hoh,' he thought. 'I wonder whether a swan can fly if he has no voice and can't say ko-hoh.'

'I think,' said the cob, 'the best plan is for me to demonstrate flying to you. I will make a short exhibition flight while you watch. Observe everything I do! Watch me pump my neck up and down before the take-off! Watch me test the wind by turning my head this way and that! The take-off must be *into* the wind – it's much easier that way. Listen to the noise I make trumpeting! Watch how I raise my great wings! See how I beat them furiously as I rush through the water with my feet going like mad! This frenzy will last for a couple of hundred feet, at which point I will suddenly be airborne, my wings still chopping the air with terrific force but my feet no longer touching the water! Then watch what I do! Watch how I stretch my long white elegant neck out ahead of me until it has reached its full length! Watch how I retract my feet and allow them to stream out behind, full-length, until they extend beyond my tail! Hear my cries as I gain the upper air and start trumpeting! See how strong and steady my wingbeat has become! Then watch me bank and turn, set my wings, and glide down! And just as I reach the pond again, watch how I shoot my feet out in front of me and use them for the splashdown, as though they were a pair of water skis! Having watched all this, then you can join me, and your mother, too, and we will all make a practice flight together, until you get the hang of it. Then tomorrow we will do it again, and instead of returning to the pond, we will head south to Montana. Are you ready for my exhibition flight?'

'Ready!' cried all the cygnets except Louis.

'Very well, here I go!' cried the cob.

As the others watched, he swam downwind to the end of the pond, turned, tested the wind, pumped his neck up and down, trumpeted, and after a rush of two hundred feet, got into the air and began gaining altitude. His long white neck stretched out ahead. His big black feet stretched out behind. His wings had great power. The beat slowed as he settled into sustained flight. All eyes watched. Louis was more excited than he had ever been. 'I wonder if I can really do it?' he thought. 'Suppose I fail! Then the others will fly away, and I will be left here all alone on this deserted pond, with winter approaching, with no father, no mother, no sisters, no brothers, and no food to eat when the pond freezes over. I will die of starvation. I'm scared.'

In a few minutes, the cob glided down out of the sky and skidded to a stop on the pond. They all cheered. 'Ko-hoh, ko-hoh, beep beep, beep beep!' All but Louis. He had to express his approval simply by beating his wings and splashing water in his father's face.

'All right,' said the cob. 'You've seen how

it's done. Follow me, and we'll give it a try. Extend yourselves to the utmost, do everything in the proper order, never forget for a minute that you are swans and therefore excellent fliers, and I'm sure all will be well.'

They all swam downwind to the end of the pond. They pumped their necks up and down. Louis pumped his harder than any of the others. They tested the wind by turning their heads this way and that. Suddenly the cob signalled for the start. There was a tremendous commotion – wings beating, feet racing, water churned to a froth. And presently, wonder of wonders, there were seven swans in the air – two pure white ones and five dirty grey ones. The take-off was accomplished, and they started gaining altitude.

Louis was the first of the young cygnets to become airborne, ahead of all his brothers and sisters. The minute his feet lifted clear of the water, he knew he could fly. It was a tremendous relief – as well as a splendid sensation.

'Boy!' he said to himself. 'I never knew flying could be such fun. This is great. This is sensational. This is superb. I feel exalted, and I'm not dizzy. I'll be able to get to Montana with the rest of the family. I may be defective, but at least I can fly.'

The seven great birds stayed aloft about half an hour, then returned to the pond, the cob still in the lead. They all had a drink to celebrate the successful flight. Next day they were up early. It was a beautiful fall morning, with mist rising from the pond and the trees shining in all colours. Toward the end of the afternoon, as the sun sank low in the sky, the swans took off from the pond and began their journey to Montana. 'This way!' cried the cob. He swung to his left and straightened out on a southerly course. The others followed, trumpeting as they went. As they passed over the camp where Sam Beaver was, Sam heard them and ran out. He stood watching as they grew smaller and smaller in the distance and finally disappeared.

'What was it?' asked his father, when Sam returned indoors.

'Swans,' replied Sam. 'They're headed south.'

'We'd better do the same,' said Mr Beaver. 'I think Shorty will be here tomorrow to take us out.'

Mr Beaver lay down on his bunk. 'What kind of swans were they?' he asked.

'Trumpeters,' said Sam.

'That's funny,' said Mr Beaver. 'I thought Trumpeter Swans had quit migrating. I thought they spent the whole year on the Red Rock Lakes, where they are protected.'

'Most of 'em do,' replied Sam. 'But not all of 'em.'

It was bedtime. Sam got out his diary. This is what he wrote:

I heard the swans tonight. They are headed south. It must be wonderful to fly at night. I wonder whether I'll ever see one of them again. How does a bird know how to get from where he is to where he wants to be?

7. School Days

A FEW days after the swans arrived at their winter home on the Red Rock Lakes, Louis had an idea. He decided that since he was unable to use his voice, he should learn to read and write. 'If I'm defective in one respect,' he said to himself, 'I should try and develop myself along other lines. I will learn to read and write. Then I will hang a small slate around my neck and carry a chalk pencil. In that way I will be able to communicate with anybody who can read.'

Louis liked company, and he already had

many friends on the lakes. The place was a refuge for water birds – swans, geese, ducks, and other waterfowl. They lived there because it was a safe place and because the water stayed warm even in the coldest winter weather. Louis was greatly admired for his ability as a swimmer. He liked to compete with other cygnets to see who could swim under water the greatest distance and stay down the longest.

When Louis had fully made up his mind about learning to read and write, he decided to visit Sam Beaver and get help from him. 'Perhaps,' thought Louis, 'Sam will let me go to school with him, and the teacher will show me how to write.' The idea excited him. He wondered whether a young swan would be accepted in a classroom of children. He wondered whether it was hard to learn to read. Most of all, he wondered whether he could find Sam. Montana is a big state, and he wasn't even sure Sam lived in Montana, but he hoped he did.

Next morning, when his parents were not looking, Louis took off into the air. He flew northeast. When he came to the Yellowstone River, he followed it to the Sweet Grass country. When he saw a town beneath him, he landed next to the schoolhouse and waited for the boys and girls to be let out. Louis looked at every boy, hoping to see Sam. But Sam wasn't there.

'Wrong town, wrong school,' thought Louis. 'I'll try again.' He flew off, found another town, and located the school, but all the boys and girls had gone home for the day.

'I'll just have a look around anyway,' thought Louis. He didn't dare walk down the main street, for fear somebody would shoot him. Instead, he took to the air and circled around, flying low and looking carefully at every boy in sight. After about ten minutes, he saw a ranch house where a boy was splitting wood near the kitchen door. The boy had black hair. Louis glided down.

'I'm lucky,' he thought. 'It's Sam.'

When Sam saw the swan, he laid down his axe and stood perfectly still. Louis walked up timidly, then reached down and untied Sam's shoelace.

'Hello!' said Sam in a friendly voice.

Louis tried to say ko-hoh, but not a sound came from his throat.

'I know *you*,' said Sam. 'You're the one that never said anything and used to pull my shoelaces.'

Louis nodded.

'I'm glad to see you,' said Sam. 'What can I do for you?'

Louis just stared straight ahead.

'Are you hungry?' asked Sam.

Louis shook his head.

'Thirsty?'

Louis shook his head.

'Do you want to stay overnight with us, here at the ranch?' asked Sam.

Louis nodded his head and jumped up and down.

'OK,' said Sam. 'We have plenty of room. It's just a question of getting my father's permission.'

Sam picked up his axe, laid a stick of wood on the chopping block, and split the stick neatly down the middle. He looked at Louis.

'There's something wrong with your voice, isn't there?' he asked.

Louis nodded, pumping his neck up and down hard. He knew Sam was his friend, although he didn't know that Sam had once saved his mother's life.

In a few minutes Mr Beaver rode into the yard on a cow pony. He got off and tied his pony to a rail. 'What have you got there?' he asked Sam.

'It's a young Trumpeter Swan,' said Sam. 'He's only a few months old. Will you let me keep him awhile?'

'Well,' said Mr Beaver, 'I think it's against the law to hold one of these wild birds in captivity. But I'll phone the game warden and see what he says. If he says yes, you can keep him.'

'Tell the warden the swan has something the matter with him,' called Sam as his father started toward the house.

'What's wrong with him?' asked his father.

'He has a speech problem,' replied Sam. 'Something's wrong with his throat.'

'What are you talking about? Who ever heard of a swan with a speech problem?'

'Well,' said Sam, 'this is a Trumpeter Swan that can't trumpet. He's defective. He can't make a sound.'

Mr Beaver looked at his son as though he didn't know whether to believe him or not. But he went into the house. In a few minutes he came back. 'The warden says you can keep the young swan here for a while if you can help him. But sooner or later the bird will have to go back to the Red Rock Lakes, where he belongs. The warden said he wouldn't let just *anybody* have a young swan, but he'd let *you* have one because you understand about birds, and he trusts you. That's quite a compliment, son.'

Mr Beaver looked pleased. Sam looked happy. Louis was greatly relieved. After a while everyone went in to supper in the kitchen of the ranch house. Mrs Beaver allowed Louis to stand beside Sam's chair. They fed him some corn and some oats, which tasted good. When Sam was ready for bed, he wanted Louis to sleep in his room with him, but Mrs Beaver said no. 'He'll mess up the room. He's no canary; he's enormous. Put the bird out in the barn. He can sleep in one of the empty stalls; the horses won't mind.'

Next morning, Sam took Louis to school with him. Sam rode his pony, and Louis flew along. At the schoolhouse, the other children were amazed to see this great bird, with his long neck, bright eyes, and big feet. Sam introduced him to the teacher of the first grade, Mrs Hammerbotham, who was short and fat. Sam explained that Louis wanted to read and write because he was unable to make any sound with his throat.

Mrs Hammerbotham stared at Louis. Then she shook her head. 'No birds!' she said. 'I've got enough trouble.'

Sam looked disappointed.

'Please, Mrs Hammerbotham,' he said. 'Please let him stand in your class and learn to read and write.'

'Why does a bird need to read and write?' replied the teacher. 'Only *people* need to communicate with one another.'

'That's not quite true, Mrs Hammerbotham,' said Sam, 'if you'll excuse me for saying so. I have watched birds and animals a great deal. All birds and animals talk to one another – they really have to, in order to get along. Mothers have to talk to their young. Males have to talk to females, particularly in the spring of the year when they are in love.'

'In *love*?' said Mrs Hammerbotham, who seemed to perk up at this suggestion. 'What do *you* know about love?'

Sam blushed.

'What kind of a bird *is* he?' she asked.

'He's a young Trumpeter Swan,' said Sam. 'Right now he's sort of a dirty grey colour, but in another year he'll be the most beautiful thing you ever saw – pure white, with black bill and black feet. He was hatched last spring in Canada and now lives in the Red Rock Lakes, but he can't say ko-hoh the way the other swans can, and this puts him at a terrible disadvantage.'

'Why?' asked the teacher.

'Because it does,' said Sam. 'If *you* wanted to say ko-hoh and couldn't make a single solitary sound, wouldn't *you* feel worried?'

'I don't *want* to say ko-hoh,' replied the teacher. 'I don't even know what it means.

Anyway, this is all just foolishness, Sam. What makes you think a bird can learn to read and write? It's impossible.'

'Give him a chance!' pleaded Sam. 'He is well behaved, and he's bright, and he's got this very serious speech defect.'

'What's his name?'

'I don't know,' replied Sam.

'Well,' said Mrs Hammerbotham, 'if he's coming into my class, he's got to have a name. Maybe we can find out what it is.' She looked at the bird. 'Is your name Joe?'

Louis shook his head.

'Jonathan?'

Louis shook his head.

'Donald?'

Louis shook his head again.

'Is your name Louis?' asked Mrs Hammerbotham.

Louis nodded his head very hard and jumped up and down and flapped his wings.

'Great Caesar's ghost!' cried the teacher.

'Look at those wings! Well, his name is Louis – that's for sure. All right, Louis, you may join the class. Stand right here by the blackboard. And don't mess up the room, either! If you need to go outdoors for any reason, raise one wing.'

Louis nodded. The first-graders cheered. They liked the look of the new pupil and were eager to see what he could do.

'Quiet, children!' said Mrs Hammerbotham sternly. 'We'll start with the letter *A*.'

She picked up a piece of chalk and made a big **A** on the blackboard. 'Now *you* try it, Louis!'

Louis grabbed a piece of chalk in his bill and drew a perfect **A** right under the one the teacher had drawn.

'You see?' said Sam. 'He's an unusual bird.'

'Well,' said Mrs Hammerbotham, '*A* is easy. I'll give him something harder.' She wrote **CAT** on the board. 'Let's see you write *cat*, Louis!'

Louis wrote *cat*.

'Well *cat* is easy, too,' muttered the teacher. '*Cat* is easy because it is short. Can anyone think of a word that is longer than *cat*?'

'*Catastrophe*,' said Charlie Nelson, who sat in the first row.

'Good!' said Mrs Hammerbotham. 'That's a good hard word. But does anyone know what it means? What *is* a catastrophe?'

'An earthquake,' said one of the girls.

'Correct!' replied the teacher. 'What else?'

'War is a catastrophe,' said Charlie Nelson.

'Correct!' replied Mrs Hammerbotham. 'What else is?'

A very small, redheaded girl named Jennie raised her hand.

'Yes, Jennie? What is a catastrophe?'

In a very small, high voice, Jennie said, 'When you get ready to go on a picnic with your father and mother and you make peanut-butter sandwiches and jelly rolls and put them in a thermos box with bananas and an apple and some raisin cookies and paper napkins and some bottles of pop and a few hard-boiled eggs and then you put the thermos box in your car and just as you are starting out it starts to *rain* and your parents say there is no point in having a picnic in the rain, that's a catastrophe.'

'Very good, Jennie,' said Mrs Hammerbotham. 'It isn't as bad as an earthquake, and it isn't as bad as war. But when a picnic gets called off on account of rain, it *is* a catastrophe for a child, I guess. Anyway, *catastrophe* is a good word. No bird can write *that* word, I'll bet. If I can teach a bird to write *catastrophe*, it'll be big news all over the Sweet Grass country. I'll get my picture in *Life* magazine. I'll be famous.'

Thinking of all these things, she stepped to the blackboard and wrote **CATASTROPHE**.

'OK, Louis, let's see you write *that*!'

Louis picked up a fresh piece of chalk in his bill. He was scared. He took a good look at

the word. 'A long word,' he thought, 'is really no harder than a short one. I'll just copy one letter at a time, and pretty soon it will be finished. Besides, my life is a catastrophe. It's a catastrophe to be without a voice.' Then he began writing. **CATASTROPHE**, he wrote, making each letter very neatly. When he got to the last letter, the pupils clapped and stamped their feet and banged on their desks, and one boy quickly made a paper aeroplane and zoomed it into the air. Mrs Hammerbotham rapped for order.

'Very good, Louis,' she said. 'Sam, it's time you went to your own classroom – you shouldn't be in my room. Go and join the fifth grade. I'll take care of your friend the swan.'

Back in his own room, Sam sat down at his desk, feeling very happy about the way things had turned out. The fifth-graders were having a lesson in arithmetic, and their teacher, Miss Annie Snug, greeted Sam with a question. Miss Snug was young and pretty.

'Sam, if a man can walk three miles in one hour, how many miles can he walk in four hours?'

'It would depend on how tired he got after the first hour,' replied Sam.

The other pupils roared. Miss Snug rapped for order.

'Sam is quite right,' she said. 'I never looked

at the problem that way before. I always supposed that man could walk twelve miles in four hours, but Sam may be right: that man may not feel so spunky after the first hour. He may drag his feet. He may slow up.'

Albert Bigelow raised his hand. 'My father knew a man who tried to walk twelve miles, and he died of heart failure,' said Albert.

'Goodness!' said the teacher. 'I suppose *that* could happen, too.'

'Anything can happen in four hours,' said Sam. 'A man might develop a blister on his heel. Or he might find some berries growing along the road and stop to pick them. That would slow him up even if he wasn't tired or didn't have a blister.'

'It would indeed,' agreed the teacher. 'Well, children, I think we have all learned a great deal about arithmetic this morning, thanks to Sam Beaver. And now, here is a problem for one of the girls in the room. If you are feeding a baby from a bottle, and you give the baby eight ounces of milk in one feeding, how many ounces of milk would the baby drink in *two* feedings?'

Linda Staples raised her hand.

'About fifteen ounces,' she said.

'Why is that?' asked Miss Snug. 'Why wouldn't the baby drink sixteen ounces?'

'Because he spills a little each time,' said Linda. 'It runs out of the corners of his mouth and gets on his mother's apron.'

By this time the class was howling so loudly the arithmetic lesson had to be abandoned. But everyone had learned how careful you have to be when dealing with figures.

8. Love

WHEN Louis's father and mother discovered that Louis was missing, they felt awful. No other young swan had disappeared from the lakes – only Louis.

'The question now arises,' said the cob to his wife, 'whether or not I should go and look for our son. I am disinclined to leave these attractive lakes now, in the fall of the year, with winter coming on. I have, in fact, been looking forward to this time of serenity and peace and the society of other waterfowl. I like the life here.'

'There's another little matter to consider besides your personal comfort,' said his wife. 'Has it occurred to you that we have no idea which direction Louis went when he left? You don't know where he went any more than I do. If you were to start out looking for him, which way would you fly?'

'Well,' replied the cob, 'in the last analysis, I believe I would go south.'

'What do you mean, "in the last analysis"?' said the swan impatiently. 'You haven't analyzed anything. Why do you say "in the last analysis"? And why do you pick south as the way to go looking for Louis? There are other directions. There's north, and east, and west. There's northeast, southeast, southwest, northwest.'

'True,' replied the cob. 'And there are all those in-between directions: north-northeast, east-southeast, west-southwest. There's north by east, and east by north. There's south-southeast a half east, and there's west by north a half north. The directions a young swan could start off in are almost too numerous to think about.'

So it was decided that no search would be made. 'We'll just wait here and see what happens,' said the cob. 'I feel sure Louis will return in the fullness of time.'

Months went by. Winter came to the Red Rock Lakes. The nights were long and dark and cold. The days were short and bright and cold. Sometimes the wind blew. But the swans and geese and ducks were safe and happy. The warm springs that fed the lakes kept the ice from covering them – there were always open places. There was plenty of food. Sometimes a man would arrive with a bag of grain and spread the grain where the birds could get it.

Spring followed winter; summer followed spring. A year went by, and it was springtime again. Still no sign of Louis. Then one morning when Louis's grown-up brothers were playing a game of water polo, one of them looked up and saw a swan approaching in the sky.

'Ko-hoh!' cried the cygnet. He rushed to his father and mother. 'Look! Look! Look!'

All the waterfowl on the lake turned and gazed up at the approaching swan. The swan circled in the sky.

'It's Louis!' said the cob. 'But what is that peculiar little object hanging around his neck by a string? What is that?'

'Wait and see,' said his wife. 'Maybe it's a gift.'

Louis looked down from the sky and spotted what looked like his family. When he was sure, he glided down and skidded to a stop. His mother rushed up and embraced him. His father arched his neck gracefully and raised his wings in greeting. Everyone shouted 'Ko-hoh!' and 'Welcome back, Louis!' His family was overjoyed. He had been gone for a year and a half – almost eighteen months. He looked older and handsomer. His feathers were pure white now, instead of a dirty grey. Hanging by a cord around his neck was a small slate. Attached to the slate by a piece of string was a white chalk pencil.

When the family greetings were over, Louis seized the chalk in his bill and wrote 'Hi, there!' on the slate. He held the slate out eagerly for all to see.

The cob stared at it. The mother swan stared at it. The cygnets stared at it. They just stared and stared. Words on a slate meant nothing to them. They couldn't read. None of the members of his family had ever seen a slate before, or a piece of chalk. Louis's attempt to greet his family was a failure. He felt as though he had wasted a year and a half by going to school and learning to write. He felt keenly disappointed. And, of course, he was unable to speak. The words on the slate were all he could offer by way of greeting.

Finally his father, the cob, spoke up.

'Louis, my son,' he began in his deep, resonant voice, 'this is the day we have long awaited – the day of your return to our sanctuary in the Red Rock Lakes. No one can imagine the extent of our joy or the depth of our emotion at seeing you again, you who have been absent from our midst for so long, in lands we know not of, in pursuits we can only guess at. How good it is to see your countenance again! We hope you have enjoyed good health during your long absence, in lands we know not of, in pursuits we can only guess at –'

'You've said that once already,' said his wife. 'You're repeating yourself. Louis must be tired after his trip, no matter where he's been or what he's been up to.'

'Very true,' said the cob. 'But I must prolong my welcoming remarks a bit longer, for my curiosity is aroused by that odd little object Louis is wearing around his neck and by the strange symbols he has placed upon it by rubbing that white thing up and down and leaving those strange white tracings.'

'Well,' said Louis's mother, 'we're *all*

interested in it, naturally. But Louis can't explain it because he is defective and can't talk. So we'll just have to forget our curiosity for the moment and let Louis take a bath and have dinner.'

Everyone agreed this was a good idea.

Louis swam to the shore, placed his slate and his chalk pencil under a bush, and took a bath. When he was through, he dipped the end of one wing in the water and sorrowfully rubbed out the words 'Hi, there!' Then he hung the slate around his neck again. It felt good to be home with his family. And his family had increased during the months he had spent with Sam Beaver at school. There were now six new cygnets. Louis's father and mother had spent the summer on a trip to Canada, and while there, they had nested and hatched six little cygnets, and in the fall they had all joined up again at the Red Rock Lakes in Montana.

One day, soon after Louis's return, the grain

man stopped by with a sack of grain. Louis saw him and swam over. When the man spread the grain on the ground to feed the birds, Louis took off his slate and wrote, 'Thank you very much!' He held the slate up to the man, who appeared surprised.

'Say!' said the man. 'You're quite a bird! Where did *you* learn to write?'

Louis erased the slate and wrote, 'At school.'

'School?' said the grain man. 'What school?'

'Public school,' wrote Louis. 'Mrs Hammerbotham taught me.'

'Never heard of her,' said the grain man. 'But she must be a darned good teacher.'

'She is,' wrote Louis. He was overjoyed to be carrying on a conversation with a stranger. He realized that even though the slate was no help with other birds, it *was* going to be a help with people, because people could read. This made him feel a whole lot better. Sam Beaver had given Louis the slate as a goodbye present when he left the ranch. Sam had bought the slate and the chalk pencil with money he had saved. Louis decided he would always carry them with him, no matter where he went in the world.

The grain man wondered whether he had been dreaming or whether he had really seen a swan write words on a slate. He decided to say nothing about it to anyone, for fear people might think he was crazy in the head.

For birds, spring is the time to find a mate. The warm sweet airs of spring stir strange feelings in young swans. The males begin to notice the females. They show off in front of them. The females begin to notice the males, too, but they pretend they are not noticing anything at all. They act very coy.

Louis felt so queer one day, he knew he must be in love. And he knew which bird he was in love with. Whenever he swam past her, he could feel his heart beat faster, and his mind was full of thoughts of love and desire.

He thought he had never seen such a beautiful young female swan. She was a trifle smaller than the others, and she seemed to have a more graceful neck and more attractive ways than any of his other friends on the lake. Her name was Serena. He wished he could do something to attract her attention. He wanted her for his mate but was unable to tell her so because he couldn't make a sound. He swam in circles around her and pumped his neck up and down and made a great show of diving and staying down to prove he could hold his breath longer than any other bird. But the little female paid no attention to Louis's antics. She pretended he didn't exist.

When Louis's mother found out that Louis was courting a young female, she hid behind some bulrushes and watched what was going on. She could tell that he was in love by the way he acted, and she saw that he was having no success.

Once, in desperation, Louis swam up to

Serena, his beloved, and made a bow. His slate, as usual, was around his neck. Taking the chalk pencil in his mouth, he wrote 'I love you' on the slate and showed it to her.

She stared at it for a moment, then swam away. She didn't know how to read, and although she rather liked the look of a young

cob who had something hanging around his neck, she couldn't really get interested in a bird that was unable to *say* anything. A Trumpeter Swan that couldn't trumpet was a bust as far as she was concerned.

When Louis's mother saw this, she went to her husband, the cob.

'I have news for you,' she said. 'Your son Louis is in love, and the swan of his choice, the female of his desiring, pays no attention to him. It's just as I predicted: Louis won't be able to get a mate because he has no voice. That snippety little female he's chasing after gives me a pain in the neck, the way she acts. But just the same, I'm sorry for Louis. He thinks she's the greatest thing on the lake, and he can't say, "Ko-hoh, I love you," and that's what she's waiting to hear.'

'Why, this is terrible news,' said the cob, 'news of the most serious import. I know what it is like to be in love. Well do I remember how painful love can be, how exciting, and, in the event of unsuccess, how disappointing and doleful the days and nights. But I am Louis's father, and I'm not going to take this situation lying down. I shall act. Louis is a Trumpeter Swan, noblest of all the waterfowl. He is gay, cheerful, strong, powerful, lusty, good, brave, handsome, reliable, trustworthy, a great flier, a tremendous swimmer, fearless, patient, loyal, true, ambitious, desirous –'

'Just a minute,' said his wife. 'You don't need to tell me all these things. The point is, what are you going to do to help Louis get himself a mate?'

'I'm leading up to that in my own graceful way,' replied the cob. 'You say that what this young female wants is to hear Louis say, "Ko-hoh, I love you"?'

'That's right.'

'Then she shall hear it!' exclaimed the cob. 'There are devices made by men – horns, trumpets, musical instruments of all sorts. These devices are capable of producing sounds similar to the wild sound of our trumpeting. I shall begin a search for such a device, and if I have to go to the ends of the earth to find a trumpet for our young son, I shall find it at last and bring it home to Louis.'

'Well, if I may make a suggestion,' said his wife, 'don't go to the ends of the earth, go to Billings, Montana. It's nearer.'

'Very well, I will try Billings. I shall look for a trumpet in Billings. And now, without further ado, I go. There is no time to lose. Springtime doesn't last forever. Love is fleeting. Every minute counts. I'm leaving this instant for Billings, Montana, a great city teeming with life and with objects made by man. Goodbye, my love! I shall return!'

'What are you going to use for money?' asked his practical wife. 'Trumpets cost money.'

'Leave that to me,' replied the cob. And with that, he took off into the air. He climbed steeply, like a jet plane, then levelled off, flying high and fast toward the northeast. His wife watched him until he was out of sight. 'What a swan!' she murmured. 'I just hope he knows what he's doing.'

9. The Trumpet

A S THE cob flew toward Billings on his powerful white wings, all sorts of troublesome thoughts whirled in his head. The cob had never gone looking for a trumpet before. He had no money to pay for a trumpet. He feared he might arrive after the shops had closed for the day. He realized that in the whole continent of North America he was undoubtedly the only Trumpeter Swan who was on his way to a city to get a trumpet.

'This is a queer adventure,' he said to himself. 'Yet it is a noble quest. I will do anything to help my son Louis – even if I run into real trouble.'

Toward the end of the afternoon, the cob looked ahead and in the distance saw the churches and factories and shops and homes of Billings. He decided to act quickly and boldly. He circled the city once, looking for a music store. Suddenly he spied one. It had a very big, wide window, solid glass. The cob flew lower and circled so he could get a better look. He gazed into the store. He saw a drum painted gold. He saw a fancy guitar with an electric cord. He saw a small piano. He saw banjos, horns, violins, mandolins, cymbals, saxophones, marimbaphones, cellos, and many other instruments. Then he saw what he wanted: he saw a brass trumpet hanging by a red cord.

'Now is my time to act!' he said to himself. 'Now is my moment for risking everything on one bold move, however shocking it may be to my sensibilities, however offensive it may be to the laws that govern the lives of men. Here I go! May good luck go with me!'

With that, the old cob set his wings for a dive. He aimed straight at the big window. He held his neck straight and stiff, waiting for the crash. He dived swiftly and hit the window going full speed. The glass broke. The noise was terrific. The whole store shook. Musical instruments fell to the floor. Glass flew everywhere. A salesgirl fainted. The cob felt a twinge of pain as a jagged piece of broken glass cut into his shoulder, but he grabbed the trumpet in his beak, turned sharply in the air, flew back through the hole in the window, and began climbing fast over the roofs of Billings. A few drops of blood fell to the ground below. His shoulder hurt. But he had succeeded in getting what he had come for. Held firmly in his bill, its red cord dangling, was a beautiful brass trumpet.

You can imagine the noise in the music store when the cob crashed through the window. At the moment the glass broke, one of the clerks was showing a bass drum to a customer, and the clerk was so startled at seeing a big white bird come flying through the window, he hit the drum a tremendous wallop.

'Bom!' went the drum.

'Crash!' went the splinters of flying glass.

When the salesgirl fainted, she fell against the keys of the piano.

'Rrrongee-rrrongee-rrrongee!' went the piano.

The owner of the store grabbed his shotgun, which went off by mistake, blasting a hole in the ceiling and sending down a shower of plaster. Everything was flying around and falling and making a noise.

'Bom!' went the drum.

'Plunk!' went the banjo.

'Rrrongee-rrrongee-rrrongee!' went the piano.

'Ump!' went the bull fiddle.

'Help!' screamed a clerk. 'We've been robbed.'

'Make way!' shouted the owner. He ran for the door, stepped outside, and fired another shot – *bang*! – at the disappearing bird. His shot was too late. The cob was safe in the sky, beyond the range of gunfire. He was headed home, toward the southwest, high above the roofs and spires of Billings. In his beak was the trumpet. In his heart was the pain of having committed a crime.

'I have robbed a store,' he said to himself. 'I have become a thief. What a miserable fate for a bird of my excellent character and high ideals! Why did I do this? What led me to commit this awful crime? My past life has been blameless – a model of good behavior and correct conduct. I am by nature law-abiding. Why, oh, why did I do this?'

Then the answer came to him, as he flew steadily on through the evening sky. 'I did it to help my son. I did it for love of my son Louis.'

Back in Billings, the news spread rapidly. This was the first time a swan had broken into a music store and made off with a trumpet. A lot of people refused to believe it had happened. The editor of the newspaper sent a reporter to the store to look around. The reporter interviewed the owner and wrote an article about the event for the paper. The article was headed:

LARGE BIRD BREAKS INTO MUSIC STORE

White Swan Crashes Through Window and Makes Off With Valuable Trumpet

Everybody in Billings bought a copy of the paper and read all about the extraordinary event. It was talked about all over town. Some people believed it; others said it never could have happened. They said the store owner had just invented it to get some publicity for his store. But the clerks in the store agreed that it had really happened. They pointed to the drops of blood on the floor.

The police came to look over the damage, which was estimated at nine hundred dollars. The police promised they would try to find the thief and arrest him, but the police were sorry to hear that the thief was a bird. 'Birds are a special problem,' they said. 'Birds are hard to deal with.'

Back at the Red Rock Lakes, Louis's mother waited anxiously for her husband to return. When he showed up in the night sky, she saw that he had a trumpet with him. It was slung around his neck by its cord.

'Well,' she said, as he glided to a stop in the water, 'I see you made it.'

'I did, my dear,' said the cob. 'I travelled fast and far, sacrificed my honour, and I have returned. Where is Louis? I want to give him his trumpet right away.'

'He's over there sitting on a muskrat house,

dreaming about that empty-headed young female he's so crazy about.'

The cob swam over to his son and made a presentation speech.

'Louis,' he said, 'I have been on a journey to the haunts of men. I visited a great city teeming with life and commerce. Whilst there, I picked up a gift for you, which I now bestow upon you with my love and my blessing. Here, Louis, is a trumpet. It will be your voice – a substitute for the voice God failed to give you. Learn to blow it, Louis, and life will be smoother and richer and gayer for you! With the help of this horn, you will be able at last to say ko-hoh, like every other swan. The sound of music will be in our ears. You will be able to attract the attention of desirable young females. Master this trumpet, and you will be able to play love songs for them, filling them with ardour and surprise and longing. I hope it will bring you happiness, Louis, and a new and better life. I procured it at some personal sacrifice to myself and my pride, but we won't go into that now. The long and short of it is, I had no money; I took the trumpet without paying for it. This was deplorable. But the important thing is that you learn to play the instrument.'

So saying, the cob removed the trumpet from around his neck and hung it on Louis, alongside the slate and the white chalk pencil.

'Wear it in health!' he said. 'Blow it in happiness! Make the woods and the hills and the marshes echo with the sounds of your youthful desire!'

Louis wanted to thank his father, but he was unable to say a word. And he knew it would do no good to write 'Thank you' on the slate, because his father wouldn't be able to read it, never having had an education. So Louis just bobbed his head and waggled his tail and fluttered his wings. The cob knew by these signs that he had found favour in the sight of his son and that the gift of a trumpet was acceptable.

10. Money Trouble

LOUIS was the best-liked young male swan on Upper Red Rock Lake. He was also the best equipped. He not only had a slate and a chalk pencil around his neck, he had a brass trumpet on a red cord. The young females were beginning to notice him because he looked entirely different from the other cygnets. He stood out in a crowd. None of the others carried anything with them.

Louis was delighted with the new trumpet. All day, the first day he had it, he tried to get it to make a noise. Holding the trumpet was

not easy. He tried several different positions, bending his neck and blowing. At first, no sound came out. He blew harder and harder, puffing out his cheeks and getting red in the face.

'This is going to be tough,' he thought.

But then he discovered that, by holding his tongue in a certain way, he could get the trumpet to emit a small gasping sound. It wasn't a very pretty noise, but at least it was a noise. It sounded a little like hot air escaping from a radiator.

'Puwoowf, puwoowf,' went the trumpet.

Louis kept at it. Finally, on the second day of trying, he got it to play a note – a clear note.

'Ko!' went the trumpet.

Louis's heart skipped a beat when he heard it. A duck, swimming nearby, stopped to listen.

'Ko! Ko ee oo oooph,' went the trumpet.

'It will take time,' thought Louis. 'I'm not going to become a trumpeter in a day, that's for sure. But Rome wasn't built in a day, and I'm going to learn to blow this horn if it takes me all summer.'

Louis had other problems besides learning the trumpet. For one thing, he knew that his trumpet wasn't paid for – it had been stolen. He didn't like that at all. For another thing, Serena, the swan he was in love with, had gone away. She had left the lakes with several other young swans and had flown north to the Snake River. Louis was afraid he might never see her again. So he found himself with a broken heart, a stolen trumpet, and no one to give him any lessons.

Whenever Louis was in trouble, his thoughts turned to Sam Beaver. Sam had helped him before; perhaps he could help him again. Besides, springtime was making him restless: he felt an urge to leave the lakes and fly somewhere. So he took off one morning and headed straight for the Bar Nothing Ranch, in the Sweet Grass country, where Sam lived.

Flying was not as easy as it once had been. If you've ever tried to fly with a trumpet dangling from your neck and a slate flapping in the wind and a chalk pencil bouncing around at the end of its string, you know how hard it can be. Louis realized that there were advantages in travelling light and not having too many possessions clinging to you. Nevertheless, he was a strong flier, and the slate and the chalk pencil and the trumpet were important to him.

When he reached the ranch where Sam lived, he circled once, then glided down and walked into the barn. He found Sam grooming his pony.

'Well, look who's here!' exclaimed Sam. 'You look like a travelling salesman with all that stuff around your neck. I'm glad to see you.'

Louis propped the slate up against the pony's stall. 'I'm in trouble,' he wrote.

'What's the matter?' asked Sam. 'And where did you get the trumpet?'

'That's the trouble,' wrote Louis. 'My father

stole it. He gave it to me because I have no voice. The trumpet hasn't been paid for.'

Sam whistled through his teeth. Then he led the pony into his stall, tied him, came out, and sat down on a bale of hay. For a while he just stared at the bird. Finally he said, 'You've got a money problem. But that's not unusual. Almost everybody has a money problem. What you need is a job. Then you can save your earnings, and when you get enough money saved up, your father can pay back the man he stole the trumpet from. Can you actually *play* that thing?'

Louis nodded. He raised the trumpet to his beak.

'Ko!' said the trumpet. The pony jumped.

'Hey!' said Sam. 'That's pretty good. Do you know any other notes?'

Louis shook his head.

'I've got an idea,' said Sam. 'I have a job this summer as a junior counsellor at a boys' camp in Ontario. That's in Canada. I'll bet

I can get you a job as camp bugler if you can learn a few more notes. The camp wants somebody that can blow a horn. The idea is, you blow a lot of loud fast notes in the early morning to wake the boys up. That's called reveille. Then you blow some other notes to call the campers to their meals. That's called the mess call. Then at night when everybody is in bed and the light has faded from the sky and the lake is calm and the mosquitoes are busy in the tents, biting the boys, and the boys are getting sleepy in their beds, you blow some other notes, very soft and sweet and sad. That's called taps. Do you want to go to camp with me and try it?'

'I'll try anything,' wrote Louis. 'I am desperate for money.'

Sam chuckled. 'OK,' he said. 'Camp opens in about three weeks. That'll give you time to learn the bugle calls. I'll buy you a music book that tells what the notes are.'

And Sam did. He found a book of trumpet

calls, such as they use in the Army. He read the instructions to Louis. 'Stand erect. Always hold the trumpet straight from the body. Do not point it down toward the ground as this position cramps the lungs and gives the performer a very poor appearance. The instrument should be cleaned once a week to remove the spit.'

Every afternoon, when the guests on Mr Beaver's ranch had gone off on pack trips in the hills, Louis practiced the calls. Pretty soon he could play reveille, mess call, and taps. He particularly liked the sound of taps. Louis was musically inclined and was eager to become a really good trumpeter. 'A Trumpeter Swan,' he thought, 'should blow a good trumpet.' He liked the idea of getting a job, too, and earning money. He was just the right age for going to work. He was almost two years old.

On the night before they were to leave for camp, Sam packed all his camping things in a duffel bag. He packed sneakers and moccasins. He packed jerseys that said 'Camp

Kookooskoos' on the front. He rolled his camera in a towel and packed that. He packed his fishing rod, his toothbrush, his comb and brush, his sweater, his poncho, and his tennis racquet. He packed a pad and pencils and postage stamps and a first-aid kit and a book that told how to identify birds. Before he went to bed, he opened his diary and wrote:

> Tomorrow is the last day of June. Pop is going to drive Louis and me to Camp Kookooskoos. I bet it will be the only boys' camp in the world that has a trumpeter swan for the camp bugler. I like having a job. I wish I knew what I was going to be when I am a man. Why does a dog always stretch when he wakes up?

Sam closed his diary, shoved it into the duffel bag with the rest of his stuff, got into bed, turned out the light, and lay there wondering why a dog always stretches when it wakes up.

In two minutes he was asleep. Louis, out in the barn, had gone to sleep long ago.

Bright and early next morning, Louis arranged his slate and his chalk pencil and his trumpet neatly around his neck and climbed into the back seat of Mr Beaver's car. The car was a convertible, so Mr Beaver put the top down. Sam got in front with his father. Louis stood tall and white and handsome in the back seat. Mrs Beaver kissed Sam goodbye. She told him to be a good boy and to take care of himself and not to drown in the lake and not to get into fights with other boys and not to go out in the rain and get sopping wet and then sit around in the chilly air without putting a sweater on, not to get lost in the woods, not to eat too much candy and drink too much pop, not to forget to write letters home every few days, and not to go out in a canoe when it was windy on the lake.

Sam promised.

'OK!' cried Mr Beaver. 'Off we go to

Ontario, beneath the open sky!' He started the car and tooted the horn.

'Goodbye, Mom!' called Sam.

'Goodbye, son!' called his mother.

The car sped away toward the big main gate of the ranch. Just as it was disappearing from view, Louis turned around in his seat and put his trumpet to his mouth.

'Ko-hoh!' he blew. 'Ko-hoh, ko-hoh!'

The sound carried – a wild, clear, stirring call. Everybody back at the ranch heard it and was thrilled by the sound of the trumpet. It was like no other sound they had ever heard. It reminded them of all the wild and wonderful things and places they had ever known: sunsets and moonrises and mountain peaks and valleys and lonely streams and deep woods.

'Ko-hoh! Ko-hoh! Ko-hoh!' called Louis.

The sound of the trumpet died away. The ranchers returned to their breakfast. Louis, on his way to his first job, felt as excited as he had felt on the day he learned to fly.

11. Camp Kookooskoos

C AMP Kookooskoos was on a small lake, deep in the woods of Ontario. There were no summer cottages on the lake, no outboard motors, no roads with cars rushing by. It was a wilderness lake, just right for boys. Mr Beaver left Sam and Louis at the end of a dirt road, and they finished their journey to camp by canoe. Sam sat in the stern and paddled, Louis stood in the bow and looked straight ahead.

The camp consisted of a big log cabin where everybody ate, seven tents where the boys and the counsellors slept, a dock out front, and a privy out back. The woods closed in all around, but there was a bare spot that had been made into a tennis court, and there were plenty of canoes in which to take trips to other lakes. There were about forty boys.

When Sam's canoe grounded on the sandy beach next to the camp dock, Louis stepped ashore wearing his slate, his chalk pencil, and his trumpet. About twenty boys rushed down to the landing to see what was going on. They could hardly believe their eyes.

'Hey, look what's here!' one of the boys yelled.

'A bird!' cried another. 'Look at the *size* of him!'

Everybody crowded around Louis, wanting to get a close look at the new camper. Sam had to push some of the boys back, to keep Louis from getting crushed.

'Take it easy, will you?' Sam implored.

That evening after supper, the director of the

camp, Mr Brickle, built a big campfire in front of the main lodge. The boys gathered around. They sang songs and toasted marshmallows and swatted mosquitoes. Sometimes you couldn't understand the words of a song because the boys sang with marshmallows in their mouths. Louis did not join the group. He stood by himself at a little distance.

After a while, Mr Brickle rose to his feet and addressed the boys and the counsellors.

'I call your attention,' he said, 'to a new camper in our midst – Louis the Swan. He is a Trumpeter Swan, a rare bird. We are lucky to have him. I have employed him at the same salary I pay my junior counsellors: one hundred dollars for the season. He is gentle and has a speech defect. He came here from Montana with Sam Beaver. Louis is a musician. Like most musicians, he is in need of money. He will wake you at daybreak with his trumpet; he will call you to meals; and at night, when you are dropping off to sleep, he will play taps, and that will bring the day to a close. I caution you to treat him as an equal and to treat him with respect – he packs a terrific wallop with one of those wings. I now introduce, for your listening pleasure, Louis the Swan. Take a bow, Louis!'

Louis was embarrassed, but he came forward and bowed. Then he raised his trumpet to his mouth and blew a long ko. When he finished, from the opposite shore of the lake there came the echo: ko-oo.

The boys clapped. Louis bowed again. Sam Beaver, sitting with the others, his mouth full of marshmallows, was delighted that his plan had succeeded. At the end of the summer, Louis would have a hundred dollars.

A boy named Applegate Skinner stood up.

'Mr Brickle,' he said, 'what about me? I don't care for birds. I've never liked birds.'

'OK, Applegate,' said Mr Brickle. 'You don't have to like birds. If that's the way you feel about it, just go ahead not-liking birds.

Everyone is entitled to his likes and dislikes and to his prejudices. Come to think of it, *I* don't care for pistachio ice cream. I don't know *why* I don't like it, but I don't. Do not forget, however, that Louis is one of your counsellors. Whether you like him or not, he must be treated with respect.'

One of the new boys who had never been to camp before stood up.

'Mr Brickle,' he said, 'why is this camp called Camp Kookooskoos? What does Kookooskoos mean?'

'It's an Indian name for the Great Horned Owl,' replied Mr Brickle.

The new boy thought about this for a minute.

'Then why didn't you just call it Camp Great Horned Owl instead of Camp Kookooskoos?'

'Because,' replied Mr Brickle, 'a boys' camp should have a peculiar name; otherwise it doesn't sound interesting. Kookooskoos is a terrific name. It is a long word, but it has only three letters in it. It has two *s*'s, three *k*'s, and six *o*'s. You don't find many names as kooky as that. The queerer the name, the better the camp. Anyway, welcome to Camp Kookooskoos. It rhymes with moose – that's another good thing about it.

'And now it's time for everybody to go to bed. You may take a swim before breakfast tomorrow, and you don't need to wear your swim trunks. Just jump out of bed when you hear the trumpet of the swan, strip off your pyjamas, race to the dock, and dive in. I will be there ahead of you to do my celebrated back-flip from the diving tower. It freshens me up for the hard day ahead. Good night, Louis! Good night, Sam! Good night, Applegate! Good night, all!'

The light was fading. The boys straggled off to their tents in the darkness. The senior counsellors sat together on the porch and smoked one last pipe.

Sam crawled in under his blankets in Tent

Three. Louis walked to a high, flat rock by the shore and stood there, waiting. When the lights were all out, he faced the camp, raised his horn to his mouth, and blew taps.

Day is done, gone the sun, From the lake, from the hills, From the sky; All is well, safe-ly rest, God is nigh.

The last note seemed to linger on the still waters of the lake. From their beds, the boys heard the beautiful sound. They felt sleepy and serene and happy – all but Applegate Skinner, who didn't care for birds at bedtime. But even Applegate was soon asleep, along with the others in his tent. He was asleep, and he was snoring. People who dislike birds often snore.

A deep peace fell over Camp Kookooskoos.

12. A Rescue

LOUIS liked to sleep on the lake. At night, after blowing taps, he would waddle down to the sandy beach by the dock. There he removed his slate, his chalk pencil, and his trumpet and hid them under a bush. Then he shoved off into the water. As soon as he was afloat, he would tuck his head under a wing. For a while he would doze and think about home and his parents. Then he would think about Serena – how beautiful she was and how much he loved her. Pretty soon he would be fast asleep. When daylight came, he would swim ashore and eat a light breakfast of water plants. Then he'd put on his things, climb on to the flat rock, and blow reveille. The boys, hearing the trumpet, would wake and rush to the dock to swim before breakfast.

After supper at night the campers would often play volleyball. Louis loved the game. He couldn't hop around as fast as the boys, but he could reach far out with his long neck and poke the ball into the air and over the net. It was very hard to get a ball past Louis – he could return almost any shot. When the boys chose sides at the start of the game, Louis was always the first to be chosen.

The boys loved camp life in Ontario. They learned how to handle a canoe. They learned to swim. Sam Beaver took them on nature walks and taught them to sit quietly on a log and observe wild creatures and birds. He showed them how to walk in the woods without making a lot of noise. Sam showed them where the kingfisher had his nest, in a hole in the bank by a stream. He showed them the partridge and her chicks. When the boys heard a soft *co-co-co-co*, Sam told them they were listening to the Sawwhet Owl, smallest of the owls, no bigger than a man's hand. Sometimes in the middle of the night the whole camp would wake to the scream of a wildcat. Nobody ever *saw* a wildcat during the entire summer, but his scream was heard at night.

One morning when Sam was playing tennis with Applegate Skinner, Sam heard a clanking noise. He looked behind him, and there, coming out of the woods, was a skunk. The skunk's head was stuck in a tin can; he couldn't see where he was going. He kept bumping into trees and rocks, and the can went clank, clank, clank.

'That skunk is in trouble,' said Sam, laying down his racquet. 'He's been to the dump, looking for food. He poked his head into that empty can, and now he can't get it out.'

The word spread quickly through camp that a skunk had arrived. The boys came running to see the fun. Mr Brickle warned them not to get too close – the skunk might squirt them with perfume. So the boys danced around, keeping their distance and holding their noses.

The big question was how to get the can off the skunk's head without getting squirted.

'He's going to need help,' said Sam. 'That skunk will starve to death if we don't get that can off.'

All the boys had suggestions.

One boy said they should make a bow and arrow, tie a string to the arrow, and shoot the arrow at the can. Then, when they hit the can, they could pull the string and the can would come off the skunk's head. Nobody thought much of *that* suggestion – it sounded like too much work.

Another boy suggested that two boys climb a tree, and one boy could hang by his feet from the other boy's hands, and when the skunk walked under the tree, the boy who was hanging by his feet could reach down and pull the can off, and if the skunk squirted, the perfume wouldn't hit the boy because he would be hanging in the air. Nobody thought much of *that* suggestion. Mr Brickle didn't like it at all. He said it was extremely impractical and furthermore he wouldn't permit it.

Another boy suggested that they get a block of wood, smear it with glue, and when the skunk knocked against it, the can would stick to the block of wood. Nobody thought much of *that* suggestion. Mr Brickle said he didn't have any glue anyway.

While everybody was making suggestions, Sam Beaver walked quietly to his tent. He returned in a few minutes with a long pole and a piece of fishline. Sam tied one end of the fishline to the pole. Then he tied a slipknot in the other end of the line and formed a noose.

Then he climbed to the roof of the porch and asked the other boys not to get too close to the skunk.

The skunk all this time was blundering around, blindly bumping into things. It was a pitiful sight.

Sam, holding his pole, waited patiently on the roof. He looked like a fisherman waiting for a bite. When the skunk wandered close to the building, Sam reached over, dangled the noose in front of the skunk, slipped the noose around the can, and gave a jerk. The noose tightened, and the can came off. As it did so, the skunk turned around and squirted – right at Mr Brickle, who jumped back, stumbled, and fell. All the boys danced around, holding their noses. The skunk ran off into the woods. Mr Brickle got up and dusted himself off. The air smelled strongly of skunk. Mr Brickle smelled, too.

'Congratulations, Sam!' said Mr Brickle. 'You have aided a wild creature and have given

Camp Kookooskoos a delicious dash of wild perfume. I'm sure we'll all remember this malodorous event for a long time to come. I don't see how we can very well forget it.'

'Ko-hoh!' cried Louis, lifting his trumpet. The lake echoed with the sound. The air was heavy with the rich, musky smell of skunk. The boys danced and danced, holding their noses. Some of them held their stomachs and pretended to throw up. Then Mr Brickle announced it was time for the morning swim.

'A swim will clear the air,' he said, as he walked away toward his cottage to change his clothes.

After lunch each day, the campers went to their tents for a rest period. Some of them read books. Some wrote letters home, telling their parents how bad the food was. Some just lay on their cots and talked. One afternoon during rest period, the boys in Applegate's tent began teasing him about his name.

'Applegate Skinner,' said one boy. 'Where did you get such a crazy name, Applegate?'

'My parents gave it to me,' replied Applegate.

'I know what his name is,' said another boy. '*Sour* Applegate. Sour Applegate Skinner.' The boys howled at this and began chanting, 'Sour Applegate, Sour Applegate, Sour Applegate.'

'Quiet!' bellowed the tent leader.

'I don't think it's funny,' said Applegate.

'His name isn't Sour Applegate,' whispered another boy. 'His name is *Wormy* Applegate. Wormy Applegate Skinner.' This suggestion was greeted with screams of laughter.

'Quiet!' bellowed the tent leader. 'I want quiet in this tent. Leave Applegate alone!'

'Leave *Rotten* Applegate alone!' whispered another boy. And some of the other boys had to pull their pillows over their heads so their snickering couldn't be heard.

Applegate was sore. When the rest period was over, he wandered down to the dock. He didn't like being made fun of, and he wanted to do something to get even. Without saying anything to anybody, he slid a canoe into the water and paddled out into the lake, heading for the opposite shore a mile away. No one noticed him.

Applegate had no business taking a canoe out alone. He had not passed his swimming test. He had not passed his canoe test. He was disobeying a camp rule. When he was a quarter of a mile from shore, in deep water, the wind grew stronger. The waves got higher. The canoe was hard to manage. Applegate got scared. Suddenly, a wave caught the canoe and spun it around. Applegate leaned hard on his paddle. His hand slipped, and he lost his balance. The canoe tipped over. Applegate found himself in the water. His clothes felt terribly soggy and heavy. His shoes dragged him down, and he could barely keep his head above water. Instead of hanging on to the canoe, he started swimming toward shore – which was a crazy thing to do. One wave hit him square in the face, and he got a mouthful of water.

'Help!' he screamed. 'Help me! I'm drowning. It'll give the camp a bad name if I drown. Help! Help!'

Counsellors sprinted to the waterfront. They jumped into canoes and rowboats and started for the drowning boy. One counsellor kicked his moccasins off, dived in, and began swimming toward Applegate. Mr Brickle raced to the dock, climbed to the diving tower, and directed the rescue operation, shouting through a megaphone.

'Hang on to the canoe, Applegate!' he shouted. 'Don't leave the canoe!'

But Applegate had already left the canoe. He was all alone, thrashing about and wasting his strength. He felt sure he would soon go to the bottom and drown. He felt weak and scared. Water had got into his lungs. He couldn't last much longer.

The first boat to get away from the dock

was rowed by Sam Beaver, and Sam was pulling hard at the oars, straining every muscle. But things didn't look good for Applegate. The boats were still a long way from the boy.

When the first cry of 'Help' was heard in camp, Louis was coming around the corner of the main lodge. He spied Applegate immediately and responded to the call.

'I can't *fly* out there,' thought Louis, 'because my flight feathers have been falling out lately. But I can certainly make better time than those boats.'

Dropping his slate and his chalk pencil and his trumpet, Louis splashed into the water and struck out, beating his wings and kicking with his great webbed feet. A swan, even in summer when he can't fly, can scoot across the water at high speed. Louis's powerful wings beat the air. His feet churned the waves, as though he were running on top of the water. In a moment he had passed all the boats. When he reached Applegate, he quickly

dived, pointed his long neck between
Applegate's legs, then came to the surface
with Applegate sitting on his back.

Cheers came from the people on the shore

and in the boats. Applegate clung to Louis's neck. He had been saved in the nick of time. Another minute and he would have gone to the bottom. Water would have filled his lungs. He would have been a goner.

'Thank God!' shouted Mr Brickle through his megaphone. 'Great work, Louis! Camp Kookooskoos will never forget this day! The reputation of the camp has been saved. Our record for safety is still untarnished.'

Louis didn't pay much attention to all the shouting. He swam very carefully over to Sam's boat, and Sam pulled Applegate into the boat and helped him into the stern seat.

'You looked pretty funny, riding a swan,' Sam said. 'And you're lucky to be alive. You're not supposed to go out alone in a canoe.'

But Applegate was too scared and wet to say anything. He just sat and stared straight ahead, spitting water out of his mouth and breathing hard.

At supper that night, Mr Brickle placed

Louis at his right, in the place of honour. When the meal was over, he rose and made a speech.

'We all saw what happened on the lake today. Applegate Skinner broke a camp rule, took a canoe out alone, and upset. He was drowning when Louis the Swan, rapidly outdistancing all other campers, reached his side, held him up, and saved his life. Let us all give Louis a standing ovation!'

The boys and the counsellors stood up. They cheered and clapped and beat on tin plates with spoons. Then they sat down. Louis looked embarrassed.

'And now, Applegate,' said Mr Brickle, 'I hope the rescue has caused you to change your opinion of birds. The first day you were here in camp, you told us you didn't care for birds. How do you feel now?'

'I feel sick at my stomach,' replied Applegate. 'It makes you sick at your stomach to almost drown. My stomach still has a lot of lake water in it.'

'Yes, but what about birds?' asked Mr Brickle.

Applegate thought hard for a moment. 'Well,' he said, 'I'm grateful to Louis for saving my life. But I still don't like birds.'

'Really?' said Mr Brickle. 'That's quite remarkable. Even though a bird saved you from drowning, you don't care for birds? What have you got *against* birds?'

'Nothing,' replied Applegate. 'I have nothing against them. I just don't care for them.'

'OK,' said Mr Brickle. 'I guess we'll just have to leave it at that. But the camp is proud of Louis. He is our most distinguished counsellor – a great trumpet player, a great bird, a powerful swimmer, and a fine friend. He deserves a medal. In fact, I intend to write a letter recommending that he be given the Lifesaving Medal.'

Mr Brickle did as he promised. He wrote a letter. A few days later, a man arrived from Washington with the Lifesaving Medal, and while all the campers watched, he hung the medal around Louis's neck, alongside the trumpet, the slate, and the chalk pencil. It was a beautiful medal. Engraved on it were the words:

TO LOUIS THE SWAN, WHO, WITH OUTSTANDING COURAGE AND COMPLETE DISREGARD FOR HIS OWN SAFETY, SAVED THE LIFE OF APPLEGATE SKINNER.

Louis took off his slate and wrote, 'Thank you for this medal. It is a great honour.'

But he thought to himself, 'I'm beginning to get overloaded with stuff around my neck. I've got a trumpet, I've got a slate, I've got a chalk pencil; now I've got a medal. I'm beginning to look like a hippie. I hope I'll still be able to fly when my flight feathers grow in again.'

That night when darkness came, Louis blew

the most beautiful taps he had ever blown. The man who had brought the medal was listening and watching. He could hardly believe his ears and his eyes. When he returned to the city, he told people what he had seen and heard. Louis's fame was growing. His name was known. People all over were beginning to talk about the swan that could play a trumpet.

13. End of Summer

A TRUMPET has three little valves. They are for the fingers of the player. They look like this:

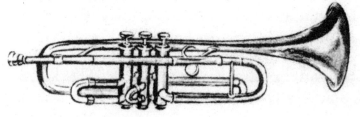

By pushing them down in the right order, the player can produce all the notes of the musical scale. Louis had often examined these three little valves on his horn, but he had never been able to use them. He had three front toes on each foot, but, being a water bird, he had webbed feet. The webbing prevented him from using his three toes independently. Luckily, the valves on a trumpet are not needed for bugle calls because bugle calls are just combinations of *do*, *mi*, and *sol*, and a trumpeter can play *do*, *mi*, and *sol* without pressing down any of the valves.

'If I could just work those three valves with my three toes,' he said to himself, 'I could play all sorts of music, not just bugle calls. I could play jazz. I could play country-and-western. I could play rock. I could play the great music of Bach, Beethoven, Mozart, Sibelius, Gershwin, Irving Berlin, Brahms, everybody. I could really be a trumpet player, not just a camp bugler. I might even get a job with an orchestra.' The thought filled him with ambition. Louis loved music, and besides, he was already casting about for ways of making money after camp was over.

Although he enjoyed life at Camp Koo-kooskoos, Louis often thought of his home on Upper Red Rock Lake in Montana. He thought about his parents, his brothers and sisters, and about Serena. He was terribly in love with Serena, and he often wondered what was happening to her. At night, he would look up at the stars and think about her. In the late evening, when the big bullfrogs were calling *trooonk* across the still lake, he would think of Serena. Sometimes he felt sad, lonely, and homesick. His music, however, was a comfort to him. He loved the sound of his own trumpet.

Summer passed all too quickly. On the last day of camp, Mr Brickle called his counsellors together and paid them what he owed them. Louis received one hundred dollars – the first money he had ever earned. He had no wallet and no pockets, so Mr Brickle placed the money in a waterproof bag that had a drawstring. He hung this moneybag around

Louis's neck, along with the trumpet, the slate, the chalk pencil, and the lifesaving medal.

Louis went to Sam Beaver's tent and found Sam packing his things. Louis took off his slate and pencil.

'I need another job,' he wrote. 'Where should I go?'

Sam sat down on his bed and thought for a while. Then he said, 'Go to Boston. Maybe you can get a job with the Swan Boat.'

Louis had never been to Boston, and he had no idea what the Swan Boat was, but he nodded his head. Then on his slate he wrote: 'Do me a favour?'

'Sure,' said Sam.

'Take a razor blade and slit the web on my right foot, so I can wiggle my toes.' He held out his foot.

'Why do you want to wiggle your toes?' asked Sam.

'You'll see,' wrote Louis. 'I need my toes in my business.'

Sam hesitated. Then he borrowed a razor blade from one of the older counsellors. He made a long, neat cut between Louis's inner toe and middle toe. Then he made another cut between Louis's middle toe and outer toe.

'Does it hurt?'

Louis shook his head. He lifted his trumpet, placed his toes on the valves, and played *do, re, mi, fa, sol, la, ti, do. Do, ti, la, sol, fa, mi, re, do.* Ko-hoh!

Sam grinned. 'The Swan Boat will hire *you,*

all right,' he said. 'You're a real trumpeter now. But with your web cut, swimming will be harder for you. You will have a tendency to swim in circles, because your left foot will push better than your right foot.'

'I can manage,' wrote Louis. 'Thanks very much for the surgery.'

Next day, the campers left. The canoes had been hoisted on to racks in the boathouse, the float had been hauled on to the beach, the windows of the lodge had been boarded up against bears and squirrels, mattresses had been packed into zipper bags; everything was snug and ready for the long, silent winter. Of all the campers, only Louis stayed behind. His flight feathers were growing fast, but he still couldn't fly. He made up his mind he would remain at camp, all alone, until he was able to take to the air again, and then he would fly straight to Boston.

The lake was lonely without the boys, but Louis didn't mind being alone. For the next three weeks he took life easy. He grew his flight feathers, dreamed of Serena by day and by night, and practiced his trumpet. He had listened to music all summer – several of the boys had radios and record players – and now he practiced the songs on his trumpet. Every day he got better and better. One day, he composed a love song for Serena and wrote the words and music on his slate:

Oh, ev-er in the green-ing spring, By bank and bough re-tir-ing, For love shall I be sor-row-ing And swans of my de-sir-ing.

He was really thinking of Serena, but he left her name out of it and kept it impersonal.

His plumage was beautiful now, and he felt great. On the twenty-first of September, he tried his wings. To his great relief, they lifted him. Louis rose into the air. The trumpet banged against the slate, the slate knocked against the moneybag, the lifesaving medal clinked against the chalk pencil – but Louis was airborne again. He climbed and climbed and headed for Boston. It was wonderful to be in the sky again.

'Flying is a lot harder than it was before I acquired all these possessions,' thought Louis. 'The best way to travel, really, is to travel light. On the other hand, I have to *have* these things. I've got to have the trumpet if I am to win Serena for my wife; I've got to carry this moneybag to hold the money to pay my father's debts; I've got to have the slate and pencil so I can communicate with people; and I ought to wear the medal because I really did save a life, and if I didn't wear it, people might think I was ungrateful.'

On and on he flew, toward Boston, which is

the capital of Massachusetts, and which is famous for its baked beans, its codfish, its tea parties, its Cabots, its Lowells, its Saltonstalls, and its Swan Boats.

14. Boston

LOUIS liked Boston the minute he saw it from the sky. Far beneath him was a river. Near the river was a park. In the park was a lake. In the lake was an island. On the shore was a dock. Tied to the dock was a boat shaped like a swan. The place looked ideal. There was even a very fine hotel nearby.

Louis circled twice, then glided down and splashed to a stop in the lake. Several ducks swam up to look him over. The park was called the Public Garden. Everybody in Boston knows about it and goes there to sit on benches in the sun, to stroll about, to feed the pigeons and the squirrels, and to ride the Swan Boat. A ride costs twenty-five cents for grown-ups, fifteen cents for children.

After a short rest and a bite to eat, Louis swam over to the dock and climbed out on the shore. The man who was taking tickets for the Swan Boat ride seemed surprised to see an enormous white swan wearing so many things around his neck.

'Hello!' said the Boatman.

Louis lifted his trumpet. 'Ko-hoh!' he replied.

At the sound, every bird in the park looked up. The Boatman jumped. Boston residents as far as a mile away looked up and said, 'What's *that*?' Nobody in Boston had ever heard a Trumpeter Swan. The sound made a big impression. People eating a late breakfast in the Ritz Hotel on Arlington Street looked up from their food. Waiters and bellboys said, 'What's *that*?'

The man in charge of the Swan Boat was probably the most surprised man in Boston. He examined Louis's trumpet, his moneybag, his lifesaving medal, his slate, and his chalk pencil. Then he asked Louis what he wanted. Louis wrote on his slate: 'Have trumpet. Need work.'

'OK,' said the Boatman. 'You've got yourself a job. A boat leaves here in five minutes for a trip around the lake. Your job will be to swim in front of the boat, leading the way and blowing your horn.'

'What salary do I get?' asked Louis on his slate.

'We'll settle that later, when we see how you make out,' said the Boatman. 'This is just a tryout.'

Louis nodded. He arranged his things neatly around his neck, entered the water quietly, took up a position a few yards in front of the boat, and waited. He wondered what would make the boat go. He couldn't see any outboard motor, and there were no oars. In the forward part of the boat were benches for the passengers. In the stern was a structure that was shaped like a swan. It was hollow. Inside of it was a seat, like a bicycle seat. And there were two pedals inside, like the pedals of a bicycle.

When the passengers were all aboard, a young man appeared. He climbed on to the stern of the boat and sat down on the seat inside the hollow swan-shaped structure and began to push the pedals with his feet, as though he were riding a bike. A paddle wheel began to turn. The Boatman cast the lines off, and as the young man pedalled, the Swan Boat slowly moved out into the lake. Louis led the way, swimming with his left foot, holding his trumpet with his right foot.

'Ko-hoh!' said Louis's trumpet. The wild sound rang loud and clear and stirred everyone's blood. Then, realizing that he should play something appropriate, Louis played a song he had heard the boys sing at camp.

> *Row, row, row your boat*
> *Gently down the stream;*
> *Merrily, merrily, merrily, merrily,*
> *Life is but a dream.*

The Swan Boat passengers were beside themselves with joy and excitement. A real live swan, playing a trumpet! Life was a dream, all right. What a lark! What fun! What pleasure!

'This is real groovy!' cried a boy in the front seat. 'That bird is as good as Louis Armstrong, the famous trumpet player. I'm going to call him Louis.'

When Louis heard this, he swam alongside the boat, took his chalk pencil in his mouth, and wrote: 'That's actually my name.'

'Hey, how about that?' yelled the boy. 'This swan can *write*, too. Louis can write. Let's give him a cheer!'

The passengers cheered loudly. Louis swam ahead again, leading the way. Slowly and gracefully, the boat circled the island, while Louis played 'Gentle on My Mind' on his trumpet. It was a lovely September morning, hazy and warm. Trees were beginning to show their autumn colours. Louis played 'Ol' Man River'.

When the Swan Boat docked and the passengers got off, long lines of people were waiting to get aboard for the next ride. Business was booming. Another boat was being made ready, to accommodate the crowds. Everyone wanted to ride the Swan Boats behind a real live swan playing a trumpet. It was the biggest happening in Boston in a long time. People *like* strange events and queer happenings, and the Swan Boat, with Louis out front leading the way, suddenly became the most popular attraction in Boston.

'You're hired,' said the Boatman, when Louis climbed out on to the bank. 'With you playing the trumpet, I can double my business. I can triple it. I can quadruple it. I can quintuple it. I can . . . I can . . . I can *sextoople* it. Anyway, I'll give you a steady job.'

Louis lifted his slate. 'What salary?' he asked.

The Boatman gazed around at the crowds waiting to get aboard.

'A hundred dollars a week,' he said. 'I'll pay you a hundred dollars every Saturday if you'll swim ahead of the boats and play your horn. Is it a deal?'

Louis nodded his head. The man seemed pleased but puzzled. 'If it isn't too much to ask,' said the Boatman, 'would you mind telling me why you're so interested in money?'

'Everybody is,' replied Louis on his slate.

'Yeah, I know,' said the Boatman. 'Everybody likes money. It's a crazy world. But, I mean, why would a *swan* need money? You can get your meals just by dipping down and pulling up tasty plants at the bottom of the lake. What do you need money for?'

Louis erased his slate. 'I'm in debt,' he wrote. And he thought about his poor father who had stolen the trumpet and about the poor storekeeper in Billings who had been robbed and whose store had been damaged. Louis knew he must go on earning money until he could pay off what he owed.

'OK,' said the Boatman, addressing the crowd, 'this swan says he's in debt. All aboard for the next ride!' And he began selling tickets. The Boatman owned several boats, all of them shaped like a swan. Pretty soon every boat was full and money was flowing in.

All day long, the Swan Boats circled the lake, carrying their load of happy people, many of them children. Louis played his trumpet as he had never played it before. He liked the job. He loved to entertain people. And he loved music. The Boatman was just as pleased as he could be.

When the day was over and the boats had made their last trip, the Boatman walked over to Louis, who was standing on shore arranging his things.

'You've done great,' said the Boatman. 'You're a good swan. I wish I'd had you long ago. And now – where are you planning to spend the night?'

'Here on the lake,' Louis wrote.

'Well, I don't know about that,' said the man uneasily. 'An awful lot of people are curious about you. They might make trouble for you. Bad boys might molest you. I don't trust the people who hang around this park at night. You might get kidnapped. I don't want to lose you. I think I'll take you across to the Ritz Carlton Hotel and get you a room for the night. It's clean, and the food is good. It would be safer. Then I can be sure you'll come to work in the morning.'

Louis didn't think much of this idea, but he agreed to go. He thought, 'Well, I've never *spent* a night in a hotel – maybe it would be an interesting experience.' So he walked along with the Boatman. They left the park and crossed Arlington Street and entered the lobby of the Ritz. It had been a long, tiring day for Louis, but he felt relieved to know that he had a good job and that he could earn money in Boston as a musician.

15. A Night at the Ritz

WHEN the desk clerk at the Ritz Hotel saw the Boatman enter the lobby followed by an enormous snow-white swan with a black beak, the clerk didn't like it at all. The clerk was a carefully-dressed man – very neat, his hair nicely combed. The Boatman stepped boldly up to the desk.

'I'd like a single room for tonight for my friend here,' said the Boatman.

The clerk shook his head.

'No birds,' he said. 'The Ritz doesn't take birds.'

'You take celebrities, don't you?' asked the Boatman.

'Certainly,' replied the clerk.

'You'd take Richard Burton and Elizabeth Taylor, wouldn't you, if they wanted to spend the night?'

'Of course,' replied the clerk.

'You'd take Queen Elizabeth, wouldn't you?'

'Of course.'

'OK,' said the Boatman. 'My friend here is a celebrity. He is a famous musician. He created a sensation in the Public Garden this afternoon. You must have heard the commotion.

He's a Trumpeter Swan and plays like the great Armstrong.'

The clerk gazed suspiciously at Louis.

'Has he any luggage?' asked the clerk.

'*Luggage?*' cried the Boatman. 'Take a *look* at him! Look at the stuff he's got with him!'

'Well, I don't know,' said the clerk, staring at Louis's possessions – his trumpet, his moneybag, his slate, his chalk pencil, his lifesaving medal. 'A bird is a bird. How do I know he hasn't got lice? Birds often have lice. The Ritz won't take anybody that has lice.'

'Lice?' roared the Boatman. 'Did you ever see a cleaner guest in your whole life? Look at him! He's immaculate.'

At this, Louis held his slate up to the clerk. 'No lice,' he wrote.

The clerk stared in amazement. He was beginning to weaken.

'Well, I have to be careful,' he said to the

Boatman. 'You say he's a celebrity. How do *I* know he's famous. You may be just kidding me about that.'

Just then, three young girls entered the lobby. They were giggling and squealing. One of them pointed at Louis.

'There he is!' she screamed. 'There he is! I'll get his autograph.'

The girls rushed up to Louis. The first girl held out a pad and pencil.

'May I have your autograph?' she asked.

Louis took the pencil. Very gracefully, he wrote 'Louis' on the pad.

More squeals, more giggles, and the girls rushed away. The clerk watched in silence.

'There!' said the Boatman. 'Is he a celebrity or isn't he?'

The clerk hesitated. He was beginning to think he would have to give Louis a room.

At this point, Louis had an idea. He lifted his trumpet and began to play an old song called 'There's a Small Hotel'.

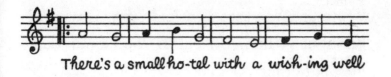

There's a small ho-tel with a wish-ing well

His tone was beautiful. Guests passing through the lobby paused to listen. The clerk leaned his elbows on the desk and listened attentively. The man behind the news stand looked up and listened. People sitting upstairs in the lounge put down their cocktails and listened. The bellboys stared and listened. For a few minutes, everything stopped in the lobby while Louis played. He charmed everyone who could hear. Chambermaids in the bedrooms paused in their work to listen to the trumpet. It was a moment of sheer magic. As the song came to an end, people who knew the words sang them softly.

> *When the steeple bell*
> *Says 'Good night, sleep well,'*
> *We'll thank the small hotel, together.*

'How about that?' asked the Boatman, grinning at the clerk. 'Is this swan a musician or isn't he?'

'He plays a sweet trumpet,' the clerk said. 'But there is one more question that I hesitate to bring up. What about his personal habits? Will he mess the room all up? Actors are bad enough. Musicians are worse. I can't allow a large bird to occupy one of our beds – it might put us out of business. Other guests might complain.'

'I sleep in the bathtub,' Louis wrote on his slate. 'Will not disturb bed.'

The clerk shifted his weight from one foot to the other. 'Who's going to pay the bill?' he asked.

'I am,' replied the Boatman. 'I'll be here early tomorrow morning when Louis checks out.'

The clerk couldn't think of any more reasons for not letting the swan have a room.

'Very well,' he said. 'Sign the register, please!' He handed Louis a pen and a card.

Louis wrote:

Louis the Swan
Upper Red Rock Lake
Montana

The clerk studied it. He seemed satisfied at last. He summoned a bellboy and handed him a key. 'Take this gentleman to his room!' he ordered.

Louis removed his medal, his trumpet, his slate, his chalk pencil, and his moneybag and handed them to the bellboy. Together, they walked to the elevators. The Boatman said goodbye.

'Sleep well, Louis!' called the Boatman. 'And be ready to come to work promptly in the morning!'

Louis nodded. The elevator door opened. 'This way, sir!' said the bellboy. They entered the elevator and waited for the door to close. A rich smell of perfume filled the air. Louis stood very still. Then he felt himself rising. The elevator stopped at the seventh floor, and the bellboy led Louis to a room, unlocked the door, and ushered him in.

'Here you are, sir!' he said. 'Would you like a window open?'

The bellboy put Louis's luggage down, snapped on a few lights, opened a window, and laid the room key on the dresser. Then he waited.

'I guess he wants a tip,' thought Louis. So he went to his moneybag, loosened the drawstring, and took out a dollar.

'Thank you very much, sir,' said the bellboy, taking the dollar. He went out and closed the door softly behind him. Louis was alone at last – alone in a room at the Ritz.

Louis had never spent a night alone in a hotel. First he walked round and around, switching lights on and off, examining everything. In the writing desk, he found a few sheets of letter paper that said:

Ritz Carlton

BOSTON

He felt mussy and dirty, so he went into the bathroom, climbed into the tub, pulled the shower curtain across, and took a shower bath. It felt good and reminded him of the water fights he used to have with his brothers and sisters. He was careful not to splash any water out of the tub. When he was finished, he stood for a while, admiring the bath mat and preening his feathers. Then he felt hungry.

On the wall of the bedroom, he found a button that said WAITER. Louis put his beak against the button and pressed hard. In a few minutes, there was a knock at the door and a waiter entered. He was nicely dressed and tried not to show surprise at finding a swan in the room.

'May I get you something?' he asked.

Louis picked up his chalk pencil. 'Twelve

watercress sandwiches, please,' he wrote on the slate.

The waiter thought for a moment. 'Are you expecting guests?' he asked.

Louis shook his head.

'And you want *twelve* watercress sandwiches?'

Louis nodded.

'Very good, sir,' said the waiter. 'Do you wish them with mayonnaise?'

Louis didn't know what mayonnaise tasted like, but he thought fast. He cleaned his slate and wrote: 'One with. Eleven without.'

The waiter bowed and left the room. Half an hour later he was back. He rolled a table into the room, placed a huge platter of watercress sandwiches on it, along with a plate, a knife, a fork, a spoon, salt and pepper, a glass of water, and a linen napkin, nicely folded. There was also a butter dish, with several pieces of butter covered with cracked ice. The waiter arranged everything carefully, then handed Louis a bill to sign. The bill said:

12 w/c sandwiches: $18.00

'Goodness!' thought Louis. 'This is an expensive place. I hope the Boatman won't be mad when he sees this supper charge on the bill tomorrow morning.'

He borrowed a pencil from the waiter and signed the bill: 'Louis the Swan.'

The waiter took the bill and stood there, waiting.

'I guess he wants a tip,' thought Louis. So he opened his moneybag again, drew out two dollars, and handed it to the waiter, who thanked him, bowed again, and went away.

Because a swan has such a long neck, the table was just the right height for Louis. He didn't need a chair; he ate his supper standing up. He tried the sandwich that had

mayonnaise on it and decided he didn't like mayonnaise. Then he carefully pulled each sandwich apart. All he really wanted was the watercress. He piled the slices of bread in two neat piles, scooped the watercress on to his plate, and had a nice supper. He did not touch the butter. When he was thirsty, instead of drinking from the glass of water, he walked into the bathroom, drew a basinful of cold water, and drank that. Then he took his napkin, wiped his beak, and pushed the table out of the way. He felt much better.

To be all alone in a hotel room gives a person a cozy feeling and a feeling of importance. Louis felt great. But soon he began feeling rather lonely, too. He thought of Sam Beaver. He thought of Camp Kookooskoos. He thought of his father and mother and sisters and brothers, back home in Montana. He thought of Serena, the swan he loved, and wondered how she was. The words of the song he had played in the lobby came back to him:

> *There's a small hotel*
> *With a wishing well;*
> *I wish that we were there, together.*

How wonderful it would be, he thought, if Serena could be here at the Ritz to enjoy the hotel with him!

The waiter had left an evening paper on a table. Louis glanced at the front page. To his amazement, he saw a picture of himself on the lake in the Public Garden with the Swan Boat. A big headline said:

BOSTON GOES WILD OVER THE TRUMPET OF THE SWAN

The news story began:

There's a new bird in town. His name is Louis. He is a Trumpeter Swan that really plays the trumpet. Incredible though it may seem, this rare and beautiful water bird has accepted employment with the Swan Boat management in the Public Garden and is entertaining boat riders with his smooth trumpet. Crowds gathered at the lake this afternoon after his arrival, and the sweet notes of his horn were heard in many parts of Boston. . . .

Louis read the article to the end and then tore it out of the paper. 'Sam Beaver ought to know about this,' he thought. From the writing desk in his room, Louis took a pen and a sheet of letter paper. This is what he wrote:

Dear Sam:

I am spending the night at the Ritz in fashionable surroundings. You were right about Boston – it is very pleasant. I was able to find work as soon as I arrived. I am associated with the Swan Boat at a salary of $100 a week. You may be interested in the enclosed clipping from today's paper. If all goes well, I'll soon have enough money to pay my father's debt to the music store, and then I will own the trumpet free and clear and will hope that by blowing it passionately I will be able to make a favourable impression on the young female I am in love with. Then everybody will be happy: my father's honour will be restored, the music shop in Billings will be repaid, and I can take a wife. I hope you are well. I miss you. A hotel room, even though it has every convenience, can be a lonely place.

Your friend,
Louis

Louis addressed an envelope to Sam, folded the letter, fitted the newspaper clipping in, and found a six-cent stamp in his moneybag. He sealed the envelope, pasted the stamp on, and dropped the letter in a mail chute outside the door of his room. 'Now I'll go to sleep,' he thought.

He went into the bathroom, used the toilet, then drew a full tub of cold water in the bathtub. He couldn't get Serena out of his mind. How wonderful it would be if only she were here! Before settling down for the night, he picked up his trumpet and played the song he had composed for her when he was in Ontario:

> *Oh, ever in the greening spring,*
> *By bank and bough retiring,*
> *For love shall I be sorrowing*
> *And swans of my desiring.*

He tried to play softly, but in a minute the phone rang in his room. Louis lifted the receiver and put it to his ear.

'I'm sorry, sir,' a voice said, 'but I'll have to ask you not to make so much noise. The Ritz does not allow its guests to play brass instruments in the bedrooms.'

Louis hung up the phone and put his trumpet away. Then he turned out the lights, climbed into the tub, curved his long neck around to the right, rested his head on his back, tucked his bill under his wing, and lay there, floating on the water, his head cradled softly in his feathers. Soon he was asleep, dreaming of little lakes in the north in the springtime, dreaming of Serena, his true love.

16. Philadelphia

LOUIS worked all the last week of September for the Swan Boat man in the Boston Public Garden. He was a great success and was becoming famous. On Saturday, the Boatman paid him a hundred dollars in cash, which Louis placed carefully in his moneybag. The Boatman, after paying the first night's bill at the Ritz Carlton Hotel, decided to let Louis sleep on the lake instead of in the hotel, and this suited Louis better. He slept with the ducks and geese on the lake, floating gracefully on the surface of the water, his head tucked under his wing.

Louis took good care of his trumpet. He kept it polished, and once a week he cleaned the spit out of it. He learned new songs whenever he could, by listening to people's radios and by attending concerts. He was very good at remembering music he had heard. He was really a natural-born musician – or, in his case, a natural-*hatched* musician.

One song he liked was 'Beautiful Dreamer, Wake Unto Me'. Whenever he played it, he thought of Serena, and always, when he finished it, the passengers on the Swan Boat clapped loudly and cheered. Louis liked applause. It made him feel lighthearted and gay.

Sometimes, at the end of the afternoon, Louis played 'Now the Day Is Over'. He made it sound sweet and sad. One afternoon, when he was leading the last trip of the day, he played the 'Cradle Song' by Brahms. The passengers sang the words:

A boy in the front seat of the boat pulled an air rifle from under his jacket and began shooting BB shots at Louis's trumpet. Whenever a shot hit the horn, it made a *pinging* sound. So the 'Cradle Song' sounded something like this:

> *Lul-la – by* (ping)
> *and good – night* (ping)
> *With ros-es be – dight* (ping)

The children on the boat roared with laughter when they heard this, but the grown-up passengers were angry. One of them seized the boy's rifle. Another went home that night and wrote a letter to the *Boston Globe* urging a stronger gun-control law.

On some afternoons, at the end of the day, people gathered on the shores of the lake to listen while Louis played taps. It was a peaceful scene, a memorable hour. The Swan Boat had never enjoyed such popularity or made such a lot of money for the owner. But Louis knew that the boats would not run all winter. In a few days, the boats would be hauled out for the season, to wait quietly for the arrival of spring.

One day, when Louis was waiting for the boat to take its passengers aboard, a Western Union messenger boy appeared on a bicycle.

'I have a telegram for the swan,' he said.

The Boatman seemed surprised, but he took the telegram and handed it to Louis, who opened it promptly. It was from a man in Philadelphia. The message said:

```
CAN  OFFER  YOU  FIVE  HUNDRED
DOLLARS  A  WEEK  FOR  NIGHTCLUB
SPOT.  TEN  WEEK  ENGAGEMENT.
PLEASE REPLY.
       (Signed) ABE ('LUCKY') LUCAS
                        HOTEL NEMO
```

Louis did some quick figuring. Five hundred dollars a week for ten weeks – that was five thousand dollars. Five thousand dollars would easily pay his father's debt to the music store.

He took his slate and wrote:

OFFER ACCEPTED. ARRIVE TOMORROW. MEET ME AT BIRD LAKE IN THE ZOO. SPLASHDOWN WILL BE AT FOUR FIFTY-TWO P.M. HOPE THIS WILL BE A CONVENIENT TIME FOR YOU.

Louis showed the message to the Western Union boy, who copied it on a telegraph blank.

'Send it collect!' wrote Louis.

The messenger nodded and rode away. Louis stepped back into the water, the boat's lines were cast off, and Louis led the way. He knew it was his last appearance with the Swan Boat, and he felt a little sad. It was a warm, quiet Sunday afternoon, the last Sunday in September. Louis played all his favourite tunes: 'Lazy River', 'Beautiful Dreamer', 'Oh, Ever in the Greening Spring', 'Now the Day Is Over', and then, as the boat neared the dock, he raised his trumpet and blew taps.

The last note echoed from the walls of the Ritz and lingered over the Public Garden. It was a sad farewell. For the people of Boston, it meant the end of summer. For the Boatman, it meant the end of the best week of business he had ever had. For Louis, it meant the end of another chapter in his adventurous life, out in the big world, trying to earn enough money to get his father and himself out of trouble. Louis slept peacefully that night, being very careful that his moneybag was safe. Next day he flew to Philadelphia to keep his appointment with Mr Lucas, the man who had sent the telegram.

Louis had no trouble finding Philadelphia. Almost anybody can find Philadelphia who tries. Louis simply rose into the air with all his things around his neck, and when he was about a thousand feet high, he followed the railroad tracks to Providence, New London, New Haven, Bridgeport, Stamford, Cos Cob, Greenwich, Port Chester, Rye, Mamaroneck, New Rochelle, Pelham, Mount Vernon, and the Bronx. When he saw the Empire State Building, he veered off to the right, crossed the Hudson River, and followed the railroad tracks to Newark and Trenton and points south. At half past four, he reached the Schuylkill River. Just beyond, he spied the Philadelphia Zoo. Bird Lake looked very attractive from the air. It was crowded with waterfowl of all kinds – ducks and geese mostly. Louis thought he also saw two or three swans.

He circled, picked an open spot, and exactly at four fifty-two he splashed down. His trumpet banged against his slate, his slate knocked against his medal, his medal rapped against his chalk pencil, and his chalk pencil

on its string wound itself around his moneybag.
All in all, the splashdown caused quite a
commotion. The ducks and geese were not
expecting anything like this to happen – a big
white Trumpeter Swan dropping down out of
the sky, loaded with personal possessions.

Louis paid no attention to the other birds.
He had a date to keep. He saw a man leaning
on the wide railing in front of the Bird House.
The man was dressed in a purple suit and
wore a Tyrolean hat. His face looked shrewd
and wise, as though he knew a great many
things, many of them not worth knowing.

'That must be Abe "Lucky" Lucas,' thought
Louis.

He swam quickly over.

'Ko-hoh!' he said, through his trumpet.

'My pleasure,' replied Mr Lucas. 'You are
right on time. The splashdown was sensational.
Welcome to the Philadelphia Zoo, which crawls
with rare mammals, birds, reptiles, amphibians,
and fishes, including sharks, rays, and other

fishlike vertebrates. Watch out for wild animals – this place is replete with them: snakes, zebras, monkeys, elephants, lions, tigers, wolves, foxes, bears, hippos, rhinos, woodchucks, skunks, hawks, and owls. I seldom come here; my work confines me to the throbbing heart of the city, among the money changers. I am under great pressure from my work. How was your trip from Boston?'

'Smooth,' wrote Louis on his slate. 'I made good time. What about my job?'

'A happy question,' replied Mr Lucas. 'The job will start on October fifteenth. The contract has been finalized. Your place of employment is a nightclub of great renown, across the river – a place of high fashion and low prices, a jumpy joint. You will be called upon to make appearances each evening except Sunday, and play your trumpet for the happy customers. Once in a while you can join a jazz group: "Louis the Swan on trumpet". The pay is very good. My spirits are lifted by thinking about the pay. Wealth and happiness are around the corner for Louis the Swan and Lucky Lucas, the great of heart. My agent's fee is ten per cent, a mere bagatelle.'

'How do I get to the nightclub?' asked Louis, who only understood about half of what Mr Lucas was saying.

'In a taxicab,' replied Mr Lucas. 'Be at the North Entrance of the Zoo, Girard Avenue and Thirty-fourth Street, at nine o'clock on the evening of October fifteenth, a night that will live in memory. A cab will await your pleasure and will transport you to the club. The driver is a friend of mine. He, too, is under pressure from his work.'

'Who's going to pay for the cab?' asked Louis on his slate.

'I am,' replied Mr Lucas. 'Lucky Lucas, the generous of heart, pays for the cab for Louis the Swan. And by the way, I see that you are wearing a moneybag and that it is plump with moola. I suggest, from the kindness of my great heart, that you turn this moneybag over to me for safekeeping during your stay in Philadelphia, a place of many thieves and pickpockets.'

'No, thank you,' wrote Louis. 'Will keep moneybag myself.'

'Very well,' said Mr Lucas. 'And now there is one other small matter I must bring to your attention. Most of the birds that swim on this luxury lagoon have undergone surgery. Candour compels me to tell you that the tip of one wing is usually removed by the management – a painless operation, popular with zoos the world over. "Pinioned" is the word for it, I believe. It detains the water bird and prevents him from leaving the narrow confines of this public park and rising into the air, because when one wing is shorter than the other, the balance of the bird is upset. His attempt to take off would be crowned with failure. In short, he can't fly. Sensing in advance the revulsion *you* would feel toward having the tip of one of your powerful wings removed, I approached the Man in Charge of Birds and laid before him a proposition. He has agreed not to clip your wing. It is arranged. He is a man of honour. Your freedom of movement is assured. You will not be pinioned. But in return for this so great favour on the part of the management of the Philadelphia Zoo, you are to give a free concert here at the lake every Sunday afternoon for the people of Philadelphia, the peasantry, who come here to refresh themselves. Is it a deal?'

'Yes,' wrote Louis. 'Will give Sunday concert.'

'Good!' said Mr Lucas. 'Farewell for the nonce! Be at the North Entrance at nine! October fifteen. A cab will await you. Play well, Sweet Swan! You will be the finest thing that has happened to Philadelphia since the Constitutional Convention of 1787.'

Louis didn't understand this, but he nodded goodbye to Mr Lucas and swam off toward

the island in the centre of the lake. There he stepped ashore, straightened his things, preened his feathers, and rested. He was not sure he was going to like his new job. He was not sure he liked Mr Lucas. But he needed money badly, and when you need money, you are willing to put up with difficulties and uncertainties. One *good thing* about the whole business was the Zoo itself. It seemed like an extremely nice place in spite of what he had heard about having your wing clipped. Louis had no intention of having a wing clipped.

'I'll sock anybody who tries *that* on me!' he said to himself.

He was pleased to see so many other water birds. There were many kinds of ducks and geese. In the distance, he saw three Trumpeter Swans. They were old residents of the Lake. Their names were Curiosity, Felicity, and Apathy. Louis decided he would wait a day or two before making their acquaintance.

Bird Lake has a fence around it. When the night came for him to start work, Louis polished his trumpet, put on all his things, flew over the fence, and landed at the North Entrance. He was there promptly at nine. The taxicab was there, waiting, just as Mr Lucas had promised. Louis got in and was driven away to his new job.

17. Serena

DURING the next ten weeks, Louis got rich. He went every evening except Sundays to the nightclub and played his trumpet for the customers. He did not like the job at all. The place was big and crowded and noisy. Everyone seemed to be talking too loudly, eating too much, and drinking too much. Most birds like to go to sleep at sundown. They do not want to stay up half the night entertaining people. But Louis was a musician, and musicians can't choose their working hours – they must work when their employer wants them to.

Every Saturday night Louis collected his pay – five hundred dollars. Mr Lucas was always on hand to receive his agent's fee of ten per cent from Louis. After Louis had paid Mr Lucas, he still had four hundred and fifty dollars left, and he would put this in his moneybag, hop into the waiting taxicab, and return to Bird Lake, arriving at around 3 A.M. His moneybag grew so stuffed with money, Louis was beginning to worry.

On Sunday afternoons, if the weather was good, crowds of people would gather on the shores of Bird Lake, and Louis would stand on the island in the middle of the lake and give a concert. This became a popular event in Philadelphia, where there isn't much going on on Sunday. Louis took the concert very seriously. By playing for the people, he was earning the right to remain free and not have a wing clipped.

He was always at his best on Sundays. Instead of playing jazz and rock and folk and country-and-western, he would play selections from the works of the great composers – Ludwig van Beethoven, Wolfgang Amadeus Mozart, and Johann Sebastian Bach – music he had learned by listening to records at Camp Kookooskoos. Louis also liked the music of George Gershwin and Stephen Foster. When he played 'Summertime' from *Porgy and Bess*, the people of Philadelphia felt that it was the most thrilling music they had ever heard. Louis was considered so good on the trumpet he was invited to make a guest appearance with the Philadelphia Symphony Orchestra.

One day, about a week before Christmas, a great storm came up. The sky grew dark. The wind blew a howling gale. It made a whining noise. Windows rattled. Shutters came off their hinges. Old newspapers and candy wrappers were picked up by the wind and scattered like confetti. Many of the creatures in the Zoo became restless and uneasy. Over in the Elephant House, the elephants trumpeted in alarm. Lions roared and paced back and forth. The great black cockatoo screamed. Keepers rushed here and there, shutting doors and windows and making everything secure against the awful force of the gale. The waters of Bird Lake were ruffled by the strong, mighty wind, and for a while the lake looked like a small ocean. Many of the water birds sought protection on the island.

Louis rode out the gale on the lake, in the lee of the island. He faced the wind and kept paddling with his feet, his eyes bright with wonder at the strength of the blast. Suddenly he saw an object in the sky. It was coming down out of the clouds. At first, he couldn't make out what it was.

'Maybe it's a flying saucer,' he thought.

Then he realized that it was a large white bird, struggling desperately to come in against the wind. Its wings were beating rapidly. In a moment it splashed down and flopped ashore, where it lay sprawled out, almost as if it were dead. Louis stared and stared and stared. Then he looked again.

'It looks like a swan,' he thought.

It *was* a swan.

'It looks like a *Trumpeter* Swan,' he thought.

It *was* a Trumpeter Swan.

'My goodness,' said Louis to himself, 'it looks like Serena. It *is* Serena. She's here at last. My prayers have been answered!'

Louis was right. Serena, the swan of his desiring, had been caught by the fierce storm and blown all the way across America. When she looked down and saw Bird Lake, she ended her flight, almost dead from exhaustion.

Louis was tempted to rush right over. But then he thought, 'No, that would be a mistake. She is in no condition at the moment to perceive the depth of my affection and the extent of my love. She is too pooped. I will

wait. I will bide my time. I will give her a chance to recover. Then I will renew our acquaintance and make myself known.'

Louis did not go to his job that night; the weather was too bad. All night, he stayed awake, keeping watch, at a slight distance from his beloved. When morning came, the wind subsided. The skies cleared. The lake grew calm. The storm was over. Serena stirred and woke. She was still exhausted, and very mussy. Louis stayed away from her.

'I'll just wait,' he thought. 'When in love, one must take risks. But I'm not going to risk everything with a bird who is too tired to see straight. I won't hurry, and I won't worry. Back home on Upper Red Rock Lake, I was without a voice; she ignored me because I could not tell her of my love. Now, thanks to my brave father, I have my trumpet. Through the power of music, I will impress her with the intensity of my desire and the strength of my devotion. She will hear me say ko-hoh. I'll tell her I love her in a language anybody can understand, the language of music. She will hear the trumpet of the swan, and she will be mine. At least, I *hope* she will.'

Usually, if a strange bird appeared on Bird Lake, one of the keepers would report its arrival to the Head Man in Charge of Birds, whose office was in the Bird House. The Head

Man would then give the order to have the new bird pinioned – have one of its wings clipped. But today, the keeper who usually tended the waterfowl was sick with the flu and had not come to work. Nobody noticed that a new Trumpeter Swan had arrived. Serena was being very quiet, anyway – she was not attracting any attention. There were now five Trumpeters on the lake. There were the original three captive swans, Curiosity, Felicity, and Apathy. There was, of course, Louis. And now there was the new arrival, Serena, still exhausted but beginning to revive.

Toward the end of the afternoon, Serena roused herself, looked at her surroundings, had a bite to eat, took a bath, then walked out of the water and stood for a long while preening her feathers. She felt distinctly better. And when her feathers were all smoothed out, she looked extremely beautiful – stately, serene, graceful, and very feminine.

Louis trembled when he saw how truly lovely

she was. He was again tempted to swim over and say ko-hoh and see if she remembered him. But he had a better idea.

'There is no hurry,' he thought. 'She's not going to leave Philadelphia tonight. I will go to my job, and when I get back from work, I shall abide near her all through the night. Just at daylight, I'll awaken her with a song of love and desire. She will be drowsy; the sound of my trumpet will enter her sleepy brain and overcome her with emotion. My trumpet will be the first sound she hears. I will be irresistible. I will be the first thing she sees when she opens her eyes, and she will love me from that moment on.'

Louis was well satisfied with his plan and began to make preparations. He swam ashore, removed his things, hid them under a bush, then returned to the water, where he fed and bathed. Then he fixed his feathers carefully. He wanted to look his best next morning, when the meeting was to take place. He drifted around for a while, thinking of all the songs he liked and trying to decide which one to play to wake Serena in the morning. He finally decided to play 'Beautiful Dreamer, Wake Unto Me'. He had always loved that song. It was sad and sweet.

'She will be a beautiful dreamer,' thought Louis, 'and she will wake unto me. The song fits the situation perfectly.'

He was determined to play the song better than he had ever played it before. It was one of his best numbers. He really knew how to play it awfully well. Once, when he played it at one of his Sunday concerts, a music critic from a Philadelphia newspaper heard him, and next morning the paper said: 'Some of his notes are like jewels held up to the light. The emotion he transmits is clean and pure and sustained.' Louis had memorized that statement. He was proud of it.

Now he was anxious for morning to come, but he still had his job at the nightclub to go to. He knew the night would be long and that he wouldn't be able to sleep.

Louis swam ashore to pick up his things. When he looked under the bush, he received a terrible jolt: his medal was there, his slate and chalk pencil were there, his moneybag was there, but where was the trumpet? His trumpet was gone. Poor Louis! His heart almost stopped. 'Oh, no!' he said to himself. 'Oh, no!' Without his trumpet, his whole life would be ruined, all his plans for the future would collapse.

He was frantic with anger and fear and dismay. He dashed back into the water and looked up and down the lake. Far off, he saw a small Wood Duck that seemed to have something shiny in its mouth. It was the trumpet, all right! The duck was trying to play it. Louis was furious. He skimmed down the lake, going even faster than he had on the day he had saved Applegate from drowning. He swam straight for the duck, knocked him on the head with a swift blow from his wing, and grabbed the precious trumpet. The duck fainted. Louis wiped the horn, blew the spit out of it, and hung it around his neck, where it belonged.

Now he was ready. 'Let the night come! Let the hours pass! Let morning come, when my beautiful dreamer wakes unto me!'

Night came at last. Nine o'clock came. Louis went off to work, riding in the cab. The Zoo quieted down. The visitors had all gone home. Many of the animals slept or snoozed. A few of them – the great cats, the raccoon, the armadillo, the ones that enjoy the night-time – prowled and became restless. Bird Lake was clothed in darkness. Most of the waterfowl tucked their heads under their wings and slept. At one end of the lake, the three captive swans – Curiosity, Felicity, and Apathy – were already asleep. Near the island, Serena, the beautiful Serena, was fast asleep and dreaming.

Her long white neck was folded neatly back; her head rested on soft feathers.

Louis got home from work at two in the morning. He flew in over the low fence and splashed down near Serena, making as little noise as possible. He did not try to sleep. The night was fair and crisp, as nights often are just before Christmas. Clouds drifted across the sky in endless procession, partially hiding the stars. Louis watched the clouds, watched Serena as she slept, and waited for day to come – hour after hour after hour.

At last, a faint light showed in the east. Soon, creatures would be stirring, morning would be here.

'This is my moment,' thought Louis. 'The time has come for me to waken my true love.'

He placed himself directly in front of Serena. Then he raised the trumpet to his mouth. He tilted his head: the horn pointed slightly upward toward the sky, where the first light was showing.

He began his song.

'Beautiful dreamer', he played, 'wake unto me . . .'

The first three or four notes were played softly. Then as the song progressed, the sound increased; the light in the sky grew brighter.

Beau - ti - ful dream-er wake un-to me

Star-light and dew-drops are wait-ing for thee..

Each note was like a jewel held to the light. The sound of Louis's trumpet had never before been heard at this early dawn-hour in the Zoo, and the sound seemed to fill the whole world of buildings and animals and trees and shrubs and paths and dens and cages. Sleepy bears, dozing in their grotto, pricked up their ears. Foxes, hiding in their dens, listened to the sweet and dreamy sound of the horn blown at the coming of light. In the Lion House, the great cats heard. In the Monkey House, the old baboon listened in wonder to the song.

Beau – ti – ful dream – er, wake un – to me . . .

The hippo heard, and the seal in his tank. The grey wolf heard, and the yak in his cage. The badger, the coon, the ring-tailed coati, the skunk, the weasel, the otter, the llama, the dromedary, the white-tailed deer – all heard, listened, pricked up their ears at the song. The kudu heard, and the rabbit. The beaver heard, and the snake, who *has* no ears. The wallaby, the possum, the anteater, the armadillo, the peafowl, the pigeon, the bowerbird, the cockatoo, the flamingo – all heard, all were aware that something out of the ordinary was happening.

Philadelphians, waking from sleep in bedrooms where the windows were open,

heard the trumpet. Not one person who heard the song realized that this was the moment of triumph for a young swan who had a speech defect and had conquered it.

Louis was not thinking about his large, unseen audience of animals and people. His mind was not on bears and buffaloes and cassowaries and lizards and hawks and owls and people in bedrooms. His mind was on Serena, the swan of his choice, the beautiful dreamer. He played for her and for her alone.

At the first note from his trumpet, she woke. She raised her head and her neck straightened until her head was held high. What she saw filled her with astonishment. She gazed straight at Louis. At first, she could hardly remember where she was. Directly in front of her, she saw a handsome young male swan, a cob of noble proportions. Held against his mouth was a strange instrument – something she had never seen before. And from this strange instrument came sounds that made her tremble with joy and with love. As the song went on, as the light grew stronger, she fell hopelessly in love with this bold trumpeter who had awakened her from her dreams. The dreams of night were gone. New dreams of day were upon her. She knew that she was full of sensations she had never had before – feelings of delight and ecstasy and wonder.

She had never seen a finer-looking young cob. She had certainly never seen *any* swan with so many personal possessions around his neck. And she had never been so thrilled by a sound before in her whole life.

'Oh!' she thought. 'Oh, oh, oh, oh!'

The song ended. Louis lowered his trumpet and bowed solemnly to Serena. Then he raised his horn again.

'Ko-hoh!' he said.

'Ko-hoh!' replied Serena.

'Ko-hoh, ko-hoh!' said Louis through his trumpet.

'Ko-hoh, ko-hoh!' replied Serena.

Each felt drawn to the other by a mysterious bond of affection.

Louis swam once rapidly around Serena.

Then Serena swam once rapidly around Louis. This seemed to amuse them.

Louis dipped his neck and pumped it back and forth.

Serena dipped her neck and pumped it back and forth.

Louis splashed a little water into the air. Serena splashed a little water into the air. It was like a game. It was love at long last for Louis; it was love at first sight for Serena.

Then Louis decided to show off. 'I'll play her my own composition,' he thought. 'The one I made up for her last summer at camp.' Again he raised his trumpet.

> *Oh, ever in the greening spring*
> *By bank and bough retiring,*
> *For love shall I be sorrowing*
> *And swans of my desiring.*

The notes were clear and pure. They filled the Zoo with beauty. If Serena had been in any doubt before, she no longer was. She succumbed completely to this charmer, this handsome musician, this rich and talented cob.

Louis knew that his plan had succeeded. His beautiful dreamer had waked, and she had waked unto him. Never again would they be parted. All the rest of their lives they would be together. Thoughts of small quiet lakes in the woods, where canebrakes grew and blackbirds sang, filled Louis's mind. Thoughts of springtime and nesting and little cygnets. Oh, ever in the greening spring!

Louis had been told once by his father what happened to deep-sea divers when they go far, far down into the ocean. At great depths, where the pressure is great and the watery world is strange and mysterious, divers sometimes experience what they call the 'rapture of the deep.' They feel so completely peaceful and enchanted, they never want to return to the surface. Louis's father had warned him about this. 'Always remember, when you dive deep,' he had said, 'that this feeling of rapture can lead you to your death. No matter how wonderful you feel down there, *don't ever forget to return to the surface*, where you can breathe again!'

Looking at Serena, Louis thought to himself, 'I think love is like the rapture of the deep. I feel so good I just want to stay right where I am. I'm experiencing rapture of the deep even though I'm right on top of the water. I have never felt so good, so peaceful, so excited, so happy, so ambitious, so desirous. If love is like this on a cold day in December in the Philadelphia Zoo, imagine what it's going to be like in spring on a remote lake in Canada!'

These were Louis's secret thoughts. He was the happiest bird alive. He was a real Trumpeter Swan at last. His defect of being without a voice had at last been overcome. He felt very grateful to his father.

Cautiously, he placed his head across Serena's long beautiful white neck. It seemed a very daring thing to do, but she seemed to like it. Then he backed away. Serena swam toward him. Cautiously, she placed *her* head across *his* neck. It rested there for a moment; then she swam away.

'What a daring thing!' she thought. 'But he seems to like it. How pleasing to know that I have found an acceptable mate – a cob I can love and respect, a cob that appears to be not only musical but also quite wealthy. Look at all those *things*!' said Serena to herself. Her eyes feasted on the trumpet, the slate, the chalk pencil, the moneybag, the lifesaving medal.

'What a gay cob!' she thought. 'What a dressy fellow!'

They swam off together toward the other end of the lake, where they could be alone. Then Louis, who was short on sleep, dozed off, while Serena ate her breakfast and fixed herself up.

18. Freedom

THE NEWS of Serena's arrival on Bird Lake had finally reached the Head Man in Charge of Birds. He went out to look at her and was delighted. Then he gave an order to one of his keepers.

'See to it that she is pinioned this morning – right away, before she flies off and leaves us. That swan is a valuable bird. Make sure she doesn't get away!'

Louis was just waking from his nap when he saw two keepers approaching Serena, who was standing on the shore near the ornamental fence. One keeper carried a large net with a long handle. The other carried surgical instruments. They were sneaking up on Serena from behind, very slowly and quietly.

Louis knew right away what they were up to. He grew hot with rage. If those men succeeded in catching Serena and cutting a wing tip, all his plans would go wrong – she could never fly away to a lonely lake with him; she would have to remain in Philadelphia the rest of her life, a horrible fate.

'This is my moment,' thought Louis. 'Nobody is going to clip my Love's wing while *I'm* around.'

He hustled over to the island and stripped for action. He chucked his trumpet and all his other stuff under a willow tree. Then he returned to the water and waited for the right time to attack.

The keeper holding the net was crawling quietly up on Serena from the rear. She did not notice him – she was just standing there, dreaming of Louis. Slowly, slowly the keeper raised his net. As he did so, Louis went into action. Lowering his long, powerful neck until it pointed straight out in front of him like a lance, he streaked across the water, straight at the keeper, his wings beating the air, his feet beating the water. In a flash, he reached the scene and drove his strong bill straight into the seat of the man's pants. It was a well-aimed jab. The keeper doubled up in pain and dropped the net. The other keeper tried to grab Serena by her throat. Louis beat him over the head with his wings, striking terrific blows and knocking the poor fellow off his feet. Surgical instruments bounced into the air. The net fell into the water. One keeper groaned and held his hand on his behind, where he had been stabbed. The other keeper lay on the ground, almost knocked out.

Serena slipped quickly into the water and glided gracefully away. Louis followed. He motioned for her to stay on the lake. Then he

raced back to the island, grabbed his trumpet, his slate, his chalk pencil, his medal, and his moneybag, flew over the balustrade, and walked boldly into the Bird House. He was still mad. He went straight to the office of the Head Man in Charge of Birds. He rapped on the door.

'Come in!' said a voice.

Louis entered. The Head Man was seated at his desk.

'Hello, Louis!' he said.

'Ko-hoh!' replied Louis through his trumpet.

'What's on your mind?' asked the man.

Louis placed his trumpet on the floor and took his slate and chalk pencil from his neck. 'I'm in love,' he wrote.

The Head Man leaned back in his chair and put his hands behind his head. His face had a faraway look. He gazed out of the window for a moment in silence.

'Well,' he said, 'it's natural that you're in love. You're young. You're talented. In a couple of months, spring will be here. All birds fall in love in springtime. I suppose you're in love with one of my young swans.'

'Serena,' wrote Louis. 'She arrived the day before yesterday. I used to know her slightly, back in Montana. She loves me, too.'

'That doesn't surprise me,' said the Head Man. 'You're a very unusual young cob. Any young female swan would fall for you. You're a great trumpeter – one of the best. I'm delighted to hear about this love affair, Louis. You and your bride can stay right here on Bird Lake and raise your family in comfort and safety, in the oldest zoo in the United States.'

Louis shook his head.

'I have other plans,' he wrote. Then he set his slate down and raised his trumpet. 'They say that falling in love is wonderful . . .' It was an old song by Irving Berlin. The room was filled with the sound of love. The Head Man had a dreamy look in his eyes.

Louis set his horn down and took up his slate again. 'I am taking Serena away with me in a day or two,' he wrote.

'Oh, no you're not!' said the Head Man firmly. 'Serena now belongs to the Zoo. She is the property of the people of Philadelphia. She came here because of an act of God.'

'It wasn't an act of God,' wrote Louis. 'It was a high wind.'

'Well, anyway,' said the Head Man, 'she's *my* swan.'

'No, she's mine,' wrote Louis. 'She's mine by reason of the power of love – the greatest force on earth.'

The Head Man became thoughtful. 'You can't take Serena from the Zoo. She will never fly again. My keepers clipped one of her wings a few minutes ago.'

'They tried to,' wrote Louis, 'but I beat them up.'

The Head Man looked surprised. 'Was it a good fight?'

'It was a fair fight,' replied Louis. 'They were sneaking up on her from behind, so I sneaked up on *them* from behind. They hardly knew what hit them.'

The Head Man chuckled. 'I wish I'd seen it,' he said. 'But look here, Louis, you've got to realize the position I'm in. I have a duty to the people of Philadelphia. Within the last couple of months, I've acquired *two* rare birds by accident – you and Serena. Two Trumpeter Swans! One arrived here blown by a gale, the other to keep a nightclub engagement. The whole business is most unusual for a zoo. I have my responsibility to the public. It is my duty as Head Man in Charge of Birds to see that Serena stays. You yourself, of course, are free to leave when you want to, because Mr Lucas insisted that you remain free when we arranged for your Sunday concerts. But in Serena's case ... well, Louis, she's got to have her left wing tip amputated. The Zoo can't afford to lose a young, beautiful, valuable

Trumpeter Swan just because *you* happen to be in love. Besides, I think you're making a great mistake. If you and Serena stay here, you'll be safe. You'll have no enemies. You'll have no worries about your children. No fox, no otter, no coyote will ever attack you with intent to kill. You'll never go hungry. You'll never get shot. You'll never die of lead poisoning from eating the shotgun pellets that are on the bottom of all natural lakes and ponds. Your cygnets will be hatched each spring and will live a long life in perfect ease and comfort. What more can a young cob ask?'

'Freedom,' replied Louis on his slate. 'Safety is all well and good: I prefer freedom.' With that, he picked up his trumpet and played 'Button up your overcoat, when the wind blows free . . .'

The Head Man smiled. He knew just what Louis meant. For a while the two remained silent. Louis put his trumpet aside. Then he wrote: 'I ask two favours. First, put off the operation on Serena until after Christmas – I'll guarantee she won't try to escape. Second, let me send a telegram.'

'OK, Louis,' replied the Head Man. And he handed Louis a sheet of paper and a pencil. Louis wrote out a telegram to Sam Beaver. It said:

```
AM  IN  THE  PHILADELPHIA  ZOO.
THIS IS AN EMERGENCY. COME AT
ONCE.  I  WILL  PAY  YOUR  PLANE
FARE. AM NOW WEALTHY.
          (Signed) LOUIS
```

He handed the telegram to the Head Man along with four dollars from his money bag. The Head Man was astounded. In all his days at the Zoo, this was the first time one of his birds had asked him to send a telegram. And of course he didn't know who Sam Beaver was. But he sent the wire and ordered his keepers to let Serena alone for a few days – which they were glad to do.

Louis thanked him and left. He returned to Serena, and they spent the day happily together, bathing, swimming, eating, drinking, and showing each other in a thousand small ways how much they loved each other.

Sam arrived at the Zoo on the day after Christmas. He was equipped as though he were going into the woods. Under one arm was a sleeping bag, neatly rolled. On his back was a rucksack containing his toothbrush, his comb, a clean shirt, a hand axe, a pocket compass, his notebook, a pencil, and some food. In his belt was a hunting knife. Sam was fourteen now and big for his age. He had never seen a large zoo. He and Louis were overjoyed to see each other again.

Louis introduced Sam to Serena. Then he opened his moneybag and showed Sam his earnings: hundred-dollar bills, fifty-dollar bills, twenty-dollar bills, tens, fives, ones, and some silver coins – a great pile.

'Goodness!' thought Sam. 'I hope she's not marrying him for his money.'

Louis took his slate and told Sam about the fight with the keepers and about how the Head Man wanted to keep Serena captive by clipping the tip of one wing. He told Sam it would ruin his life if Serena were to lose the power to fly. He explained that as soon as his father's debts were paid and the trumpet honestly belonged to him, he and Serena intended to leave civilization and return to a wild life. 'The sky,' he wrote on his slate, 'is my living room. The woods are my parlour. The lonely lake is my bath. I can't remain behind a fence all my life. Neither can Serena – she's not built that way. Somehow or other we must persuade the Head Man to let Serena go.'

Sam stretched out on the shore of Bird Lake and clasped his hands behind his head. He looked up at the great wide sky. It was a clear blue, with small white clouds floating slowly across. Sam knew how Louis felt about freedom. For a long time he lay there, thinking. Ducks and geese swam slowly by, back and forth, an endless procession of captive birds. They seemed happy and well. Curiosity, Felicity, and Apathy – the three Trumpeters – swam by and peered at the strange boy lying on the ground. Finally Sam sat up.

'Listen, Louis,' he said. 'How's this for an idea? You and Serena intend to raise a family every year, don't you?'

'Certainly,' replied Louis on his slate.

'OK,' said Sam. 'In every family of cygnets, there is always one that needs special care and protection. Bird Lake would be a perfect place for this one little swan that needs extra security. This is a beautiful lake, Louis. This is a great zoo. If I can persuade the Head Man to let Serena remain free, would you be willing to donate one of your cygnets, now and then, if the Zoo needs another swan for the lake? If you agree, I'll go right in and see the Head Man about the matter.'

It was now Louis's turn to think and think. After five minutes, he picked up his slate.

'Very well,' he wrote. 'It's a deal.'

Then he picked up his trumpet. 'Oh, ever in the greening spring,' he played. 'By bank and bough retiring . . .'

The waterfowl stopped swimming and listened. The keepers stopped what they were doing and listened. Sam listened. The Head Man in his office in the Bird House laid down his pencil, leaned back in his chair, and listened. The sound of Louis's horn was in the air, and the whole world seemed better and brighter and wilder and freer and happier and dreamier.

'That's a good tune,' said Sam. 'What is it?'

'Oh, just something I made up myself,' wrote Louis on his slate.

19. A Talk About Money

IN ALMOST everyone's life there is one event that changes the whole course of his existence. The day Sam Beaver visited the Philadelphia Zoo was the turning point in his life. Up until that day, he had not been able to decide what he wanted to be when he grew up. The minute he saw the Zoo, all his doubts vanished. He knew he wanted to work in a zoo. Sam loved every living thing, and a zoo is a great storehouse of living things – it has just about every creature that creeps or crawls or jumps or runs or flies or hides.

Sam was eager to see them all. But he had Louis's problem to solve first. He must save Serena from captivity. So he picked up his rucksack and his sleeping bag and walked into the Bird House and entered the office. He walked tall and straight, as though he were on a forest trail. The Head Man liked Sam's appearance and noticed that he looked a little like an Indian.

'So you're Sam Beaver,' said the Head Man, as Sam advanced on him.

'Why did you come here?' asked the Head Man.

'To defend freedom,' replied Sam. 'I heard you intended to clip the wing of a swan. I'm here to ask you not to do it.'

Sam sat down, and they talked for a whole hour. Sam assured the Head Man that Louis was an old friend. He told about discovering the swan's nest almost three years ago in Canada, about how Louis came into the world lacking a voice, about Louis's attending school in Montana and learning to read and write, about the theft of the trumpet by Louis's father, the old cob, and about Camp Kookooskoos and the Swan Boat in Boston.

The Head Man listened with great attention, but he wasn't sure he believed a word of this strange tale.

Then Sam explained his proposal for allowing Serena to go free instead of making a captive bird out of her. He said he thought it would be a good arrangement for the Zoo, because any time they wanted a young Trumpeter Swan, Louis would give them one of his cygnets. The Head Man was fascinated.

'You mean to say you came all the way to Philadelphia to help a bird?'

'Yes, sir,' replied Sam. 'I would go anywhere to help a bird. Besides, Louis is special. He's an old friend. We went to the same school. You've got to admit he's quite a bird.'

'He sure is,' said the Head Man. 'His Sunday afternoon concerts have been the biggest attraction the Zoo has ever had. We had a gorilla once named Bamboo – he's dead now. Bamboo was great, but Louis draws even more of a crowd than Bamboo did. We have sea lions that draw big crowds, but nothing to compare with Louis when he plays that horn on Sunday afternoons. People go crazy. And music is good for the animals, too – it soothes them, and they forget the cares of the day. I'm going to miss Louis when he's gone. The whole Zoo will miss him terribly. I wish he'd stay and keep his bride right here – it would be just great.'

'Louis would pine away in captivity. He would die,' replied Sam. 'He needs wild places – little ponds, swamps, cattails, red-winged blackbirds in the spring, the chorus of the frogs, the cry of the loon at night. Louis is following a dream. We must all follow a dream. Please let Serena go, sir! Please don't clip her wing!'

The Head Man closed his eyes. He was

thinking of little lakes deep in the woods, of the colour of bulrushes, of the sounds of night and the chorus of frogs. He was thinking of swans' nests, and eggs, and the hatching of eggs, and the cygnets following their father in single file. He was thinking of dreams he had had as a young man.

'All right,' he said, suddenly. 'Serena can go. We will not clip her wing. But how can I be sure that Louis will bring me a young Trumpeter Swan when I need one? How do I know he's honest?'

'He's an honourable bird,' said Sam. 'If he weren't honest and true to his word, he wouldn't have bothered to go out and earn a lot of money to pay the storekeeper back for the trumpet his father swiped.'

'How much money has Louis got, anyway?' asked the Head Man.

'He's got four thousand six hundred and ninety-one dollars and sixty-five cents,' said Sam. 'We just counted it a few minutes ago.

He received one hundred dollars from Camp Kookooskoos for playing bugle calls, and all he spent was sixty cents for postage stamps. So he arrived in Boston with ninety-nine dollars and forty cents. Then the Swan Boat man paid him a hundred dollars for one week's work, but he spent three dollars in tips at the hotel where he spent a night. So he had a hundred and ninety-six dollars and forty cents when he got to Philadelphia. The nightclub paid him five hundred dollars a week for ten weeks, which came to five thousand dollars, but he had to pay his agent ten per cent of the five thousand dollars, and he also spent seventy-five cents for some new chalk pencils and four dollars to send the telegram to me. So that makes a total of four thousand six hundred and ninety-one dollars and sixty-five cents. It's a lot of money for a bird.'

'It sure is,' said the Head Man. 'It sure is.'

'But he is going to pay my aeroplane fare

from Montana to Philadelphia and back again. That will bring the total down to four thousand four hundred and twenty dollars and seventy-eight cents.'

The Head Man looked staggered by these figures.

'It's *still* a lot of money for a bird,' he said. 'What's he going to do with it all?'

'He will give it to his father, the old cob.'

'And what's *he* going to do with it?'

'He will fly back to the music store in Billings and give it to the owner, to pay for the stolen trumpet.'

'Give *all* of it?'

'Yes.'

'But a trumpet isn't worth four thousand four hundred and twenty dollars and seventy-eight cents.'

'I know,' said Sam. 'But there was some damage to the store itself. The old cob was going like the dickens when he crashed through the plate-glass window. He shook things up pretty badly.'

'Yes,' said the Head Man. 'But it *still* wouldn't take all that money to make things right.'

'I guess not,' said Sam. 'But Louis has no use for money any more, so he's going to turn it all over to the owner of the music store.'

The subject of money seemed to interest the Head Man greatly. He thought how pleasant it would be not to have any more use for money. He leaned back in his chair. He found it hard to believe that one of his swans had been able to save more than four thousand dollars and that the money was right out there, hanging around his neck in a moneybag.

'When it comes to money,' he said, 'birds have it easier than men do. When a bird earns some money, it's almost all clear profit. A bird doesn't have to go to a supermarket and buy a dozen eggs and a pound of butter and two rolls of paper towels and a TV dinner and a can of Ajax and a can of tomato juice and a pound and a half of ground round steak and a can of sliced peaches and two quarts of fat-free milk and a bottle of stuffed olives. A bird doesn't have to pay rent on a house, or interest on a mortgage. A bird doesn't insure its life with an insurance company and then have to pay premiums on the policy. A bird doesn't own a car and buy petrol and oil and pay for repairs on the car and take the car to a car wash and pay to get it washed. Animals and birds are lucky. They don't keep acquiring things, the way men do. You can teach a monkey to drive a motorcycle, but I have never known a monkey to go out and *buy* a motorcycle.'

'That's right,' replied Sam. 'But some animals do like to acquire things, even though they don't pay anything for them.'

'Such as?' asked the Head Man.

'A rat,' said Sam. 'A rat will fix up a home for himself, but then he'll bring home all sorts

of little objects – trinkets and stuff. Anything he can find that catches his eye.'

'You're right,' said the Head Man. 'You're absolutely right, Sam. You seem to know quite a lot about animals.'

'I like animals,' said Sam. 'I love to watch them.'

'Then come with me and we'll explore the Zoo,' said the Head Man, getting up from his chair. 'I don't feel like working any more today. I'll show you the Zoo.' And away they went, the two of them.

That night Sam slept in the Head Man's office, by special permission. He unrolled his sleeping bag on the floor and crawled in. The plane taking him back home would leave in the morning. Sam's head was full of everything he had seen in the Zoo. And before he turned out the light he took his notebook out of his rucksack and wrote a poem. This is what he wrote:

SAM BEAVER'S POEM

Of all the places on land and sea,
Philadelphia's zoo is the place for me.
There's plenty to eat and a lot to do,
There's a Frigate Bird and a tiny Shrew;
There's a Vesper Rat and a Two-toed Sloth,
And it's fair to say that I like them both.
There's a Canada Goose and a Polar Bear
And things that come from Everywhere.
There are lots of things that you've never
  seen
Like the Kinkajou and the Wolverine.
You really have to go to the zoo
To see a newborn Wallaroo
Or a Fallow Deer or a White-tailed Gnu.
There are wondrous birds on a beautiful
  lake,
There's a Timber Wolf and a Hognose Snake.
There are animals with great appeal,
Like the Hummingbird and the Harbour
  Seal.
There are pony rides, there are birds of prey,

And something happening every day.
There are Wolves and Foxes, Hawks and
　Owls,
And a great big pit where the Lion prowls.
There are quiet pools and pleasant cages,
Where Reptiles lie and the Tiger rages.
The houses are clean, the keepers are kind,
And one Baboon has a pink behind.
The entire aim of a well-kept zoo
Is to bring the animal world to You.

　　　　　　　　　　　(signed) Sam Beaver

Sam left the poem on the Head Man's desk.

　Early the next morning, long before the Zoo people came to work, Sam left Philadelphia by plane. Louis and Serena went along with him to the airport. They wanted to wave goodbye. They also planned to leave Philadelphia, right then and there, and fly back to Montana. When the airport officials saw two big white birds out on the airstrip, they raised a terrible fuss. The men in the control tower sent warning messages to the pilots of incoming planes. Members of the ground crew came piling out of buildings and rushed toward Louis and Serena to chase them away. Sam was sitting by a window inside his plane, ready for takeoff, and he saw the whole thing.

Louis grabbed his trumpet.

'Off we go,' he played, 'into the wild blue yonder!' The notes carried across the airport and startled everyone. 'Ko-hoh! Ko-hoh!' called Louis. He put his trumpet away and started racing down the airstrip, with Serena racing after him. Just then, Sam's plane started into the wind for the takeoff. The two swans flew alongside. They were in the air before the plane was, and flying fast. Sam waved from the window. Louis's lifesaving medal gleamed in the morning sun. The plane rose and started to climb. Louis and Serena climbed fast, too.

'Goodbye, Philadelphia!' thought Louis. 'Goodbye, Bird Lake! Goodbye, nightclub!'

The plane, with its greater speed, gained on the swans. They began to drop behind. For a little while they headed west, following the plane. Then Louis motioned to Serena that he was going to change course. He banked to the left and swung toward the south.

'We'll go home by the southern route and take our time about it,' he said to himself.

And that's what they did. They flew south across Maryland and Virginia. They flew south across the Carolinas. They spent a night in Yemassee and saw huge oak trees with moss hanging from their branches. They visited the great swamps of Georgia and saw the alligator and listened to the mockingbird. They flew across Florida and spent a few days in a bayou where doves moaned in the cedars and little lizards crawled in the sun. They turned west into Louisiana. Then they turned north toward their home in Upper Red Rock Lake.

What a triumphant return it would be!

When he left Montana, Louis had been penniless. Now he was rich. When he left, he had been unknown. Now he was famous. When he left, he had been alone in the world. Now he had his bride by his side – the swan that he loved. His medal was around his neck, his precious trumpet dangled in the breeze, his hard-earned money was in the bag. He had accomplished what he had set out to do. All in a few short months!

Freedom felt so wonderful! Love felt so good!

20. Billings

ON A BRIGHT clear day in January, Louis and Serena came home to the Red Rock Lakes. From among the thousands of waterfowl, they quickly found the members of their own families – their fathers and mothers and sisters and brothers. It was a noisy homecoming. Everybody wanted to say hello at once. Ko-hoh, ko-hoh, ko-hoh! The wanderers were home at last.

Louis's father, the old cob, made a graceful speech – rather long, but sincere.

Louis raised his trumpet and played 'There's

no place like home. Home, home sweet home!' There was a great deal of gossip among the waterfowl about Louis's having persuaded Serena to be his wife. Everybody congratulated the happy couple. And all the brothers and sisters of Louis and Serena gathered around and looked at Louis's possessions. They were much impressed by his worldly goods. They liked the lifesaving medal, they loved the sound of the trumpet, and they were eager to see the money in the moneybag. But Louis did not open the bag. Instead, he took his father and mother to one side. They all three stepped out on shore, where Louis slipped the moneybag off his neck and, with a bow, handed it to the old cob. Four thousand four hundred and twenty dollars and seventy-eight cents.

Then Louis took his slate and wrote a note to the owner of the music store in Billings so his father would have something to show him when he got there. The note said:

To the Storekeeper of Billings:
Enclosed please find $4,420.78. It will
pay you for the trumpet and the damage to
the store.
Sorry about the inconvenience this has
caused you.

The old cob was not able to count money, and
he was not able to read, but he took the
moneybag and the slate and hung them around
his neck. He felt sure he could now pay his
debt for the stolen trumpet.

'I shall go,' he said to his wife. 'I shall redeem
my honour. I shall return to Billings, the
scene of my crime – a great city, teeming with
life –'

'We've heard that before,' remarked his wife.
'Just take the money and the note and beat it
for Billings as fast as you can go. And when
you get there, for heaven's sakes be careful!
The owner of that music store has a gun. He
will remember that the last time he saw a swan

coming at him he got robbed. So watch yourself! You're on a dangerous mission.'

'Danger!' said the old cob. 'Danger! I *welcome* danger and adventure. Danger is my middle name. I would risk my life to redeem my honour and recapture my sense of decency. I shall pay my debt and blot out the foul mark that sullies my good name. I shall rid myself forever of the shame that comes from thievery and wrongdoing. I shall –'

'If you don't stop talking,' said his wife, 'you won't get to Billings before the stores close.'

'You are right, as usual,' replied the cob. He adjusted the moneybag and the slate for flight. Then he took off into the air and headed toward the northeast, flying fast and high. His wife and son watched him until he faded from view.

'What a swan!' said his wife. 'You have a good father, Louis. I hope nothing happens to him. To tell you the truth, I'm worried.'

The old cob flew fast and far. When he spied the churches and factories and shops and homes of Billings, he circled once, then began his downward glide – straight for the music store.

'My hour has come,' he said to himself. 'My moment of truth is at hand. I shall soon be out of debt, out from under the cloud of shame and dishonour that has cast a shadow over my life for lo these many months.'

The cob had been seen already by people down below. One of the salesmen in the music store was standing by the front window, looking out. When he saw the big white bird approaching, he yelled to the storekeeper: 'Large bird approaching. Get your gun!'

The storekeeper grabbed his shotgun and raced to the sidewalk. The cob was low in the sky, gliding straight for the store.

The storekeeper raised his gun. He fired both barrels in quick succession. The old cob felt a twinge of pain in his left shoulder. Thoughts of death filled his mind. Looking back, he saw a bright red drop of blood staining his breast. But he kept going, straight for the storekeeper.

'The end is near,' he said to himself. 'I shall die in the performance of duty. I have only a few moments remaining to live. Man, in his folly, has given me a mortal wound. The red blood flows in a steady trickle from my veins. My strength fails. But even in death's final hour, I shall deliver the money for the trumpet. Goodbye, life! Goodbye, beautiful world! Goodbye, little lakes in the north! Farewell, springtimes I have known, with their passion and ardour! Farewell, loyal wife and loving sons and daughters! I, who am about to die, salute you. I must die gracefully, as only a swan can.'

With that, he sank to the sidewalk, held out the moneybag and the slate to the astonished storekeeper, and fainted away at the sight of his own blood. He lay limp on the sidewalk, to all appearances a dying swan.

A crowd quickly gathered.

'What's this?' exclaimed the storekeeper, bending over the bird. 'What's going on here?'

He quickly read the note on the slate. Then he tore open the moneybag and began pulling out hundred-dollar bills and fifty-dollar bills.

A policeman hurried to the scene and started to hold the crowd back.

'Stand back!' he shouted. 'The swan is wounded. Give him air!'

'He's dead,' said a little boy. 'The bird is dead.'

'He *is not* dead,' said the salesman. 'He's scared.'

'Call an ambulance!' screamed a lady in the crowd.

A small pool of blood formed under the neck of the old cob. He seemed lifeless. Just then a game warden appeared.

'Who shot this bird?' he demanded.

'I did,' said the storekeeper.

'Then you're under arrest,' said the warden.

'What for?' asked the storekeeper.

'For shooting a Trumpeter Swan. These birds are protected by law. You can't pull a gun on a wild swan.'

'Well,' replied the storekeeper, 'you can't arrest *me*, either. I happen to know this bird.

He's a thief. *He's* the one you should arrest.
He's been here before, and he stole a trumpet
from my store.'

'Call an ambulance!' cried the lady.

'What's that you've got in your hand?'
asked the policeman. The storekeeper quickly

stuffed the money back into the moneybag and held the bag and the slate behind his back.

'Come on, show it to me!' said the cop.

'I want to see it, too,' said the warden.

'We *all* want to see it!' cried a fellow in the crowd. 'What's in that bag?'

The storekeeper sheepishly handed the moneybag and the slate to the game warden. The warden stood straight, put on his glasses, and read the note in a loud voice: 'To the Storekeeper of Billings: Enclosed please find four thousand four hundred and twenty dollars and seventy-eight cents. It will pay you for the trumpet and the damage to the store. Sorry about the inconvenience this has caused you.'

At the mention of the sum of money, the crowd gasped. Everyone started talking at once.

'Call an ambulance!' screamed the lady.

'I'll have to take that money to the station house,' said the policeman. 'This is a complicated case. Anything that involves money is complex. I'll take the money and keep it safe until the matter is decided.'

'No, you won't!' said the game warden. 'The money is mine.'

'Why?' asked the policeman.

'Because,' replied the warden.

'Because *what*?' asked the policeman.

'Because the law says the bird is in my custody. The money was on the bird. Therefore, the money goes to me until this is settled.'

'Oh, no, you don't!' said the storekeeper, angrily. 'The money is mine. It says so right here on this slate. The four thousand four hundred and twenty dollars and seventy-eight cents is mine. Nobody's going to take it away from me.'

'Yes, they are!' said the policeman. '*I* am.'

'No, *I* am,' said the game warden.

'Is there a lawyer in the crowd?' asked the storekeeper. 'We'll settle this matter right here and now.'

A tall man stepped forward.

'I'm Judge Ricketts,' he said. 'I'll decide this case. Now then, who saw the bird arrive?'

'I did,' said the salesman.

'Call an ambulance!' screamed the lady.

'I saw the bird, too,' said a small boy named Alfred Gore.

'OK,' said the judge. 'Describe what happened, exactly as you saw it.'

The salesman spoke first. 'Well,' he said, 'I was looking out the window and saw a swan approaching. So I hollered. The boss got his gun and fired, and the bird fell to the sidewalk. There was a drop or two of blood.'

'Did you notice anything special about the bird?' asked Judge Ricketts.

'He carried money,' replied the salesman. 'You don't often see any money on a bird, so I noticed it.'

'All right,' said the judge. 'Now we'll let Alfred Gore tell it as *he* saw it. Describe what you saw, Alfred!'

'Well,' said the little boy, 'I was very thirsty, and so I wanted to go to a candy store and get something to drink.'

'Just tell what you saw, please, Alfred,' said the judge. 'Never mind how thirsty you were.'

'I was coming along the street,' continued Alfred, 'because I was very thirsty. So I was coming along the street on my way to the candy store to get something to drink, and there, up in the sky, all of a sudden there was a big white bird right over me in the sky and he was sliding down out of the sky like *this*.' Alfred held out his arms and imitated a bird. 'And so when I saw the big bird I stopped thinking about how thirsty I was and pretty soon this enormous bird, he was enormous, was on the sidewalk and he was dead and there was blood all over everything and that's what I saw.'

'Did you notice anything special about the bird?' asked Judge Ricketts.

'Blood,' said Alfred.

'Anything else?'

'No, just blood.'

'Did you hear a gun?'

'No, just blood,' said Alfred.

'Thank you!' said the judge. 'That will be all.'

Just then a siren started wailing – woooaw, woooaw, woooaw. An ambulance came screaming down the street. It stopped in front of the crowd. Two men jumped out. They carried a stretcher and set it down next to where the swan lay. The old cob lifted his head and looked around. 'I have been at death's door,' he thought, 'and now I think I am returning to life. I am reviving. I shall live! I shall return on strong wings to the great sky. I shall glide gracefully again on the ponds of the world and hear the frogs and take pleasure in the sounds of night and the coming of day.'

As he was thinking these pleasant thoughts, he felt himself being lifted. The ambulance attendants put his slate around his neck, picked him up, laid him gently on the stretcher, and carried him into the ambulance, which had a red light whirling round and around on top of it. One of the men placed an oxygen mask over the old cob's head and gave him some oxygen. And away they drove, making a great deal of noise, to the hospital. There, he was put to bed and given a shot of penicillin. A young doctor came in and examined the wound where the shotgun pellet had hit him. The doctor said the wound was superficial. The old cob didn't know what 'superficial' meant, but it sounded serious.

Nurses gathered around. One of them took the swan's blood pressure and wrote something on a chart. The old cob was beginning to feel very well again. It felt good to be in bed, being cared for by nurses – one of whom was quite pretty. The doctor washed the wound and put a Band-Aid on it.

Meantime, back on the sidewalk in front of the music store, the judge was announcing his decision.

'On the basis of the testimony,' he said solemnly, 'I award the money to the storekeeper, to make up for the loss of the trumpet and damage to the store. I am placing the swan in the custody of the game warden.'

'Your Honour,' said the warden, 'don't forget that the storekeeper is under arrest for shooting a wild swan.'

'It was a case of false arrest,' said the judge wisely. 'The storekeeper fired his gun at the bird because he was afraid his store would be robbed again. He did not know that the swan was bringing money to pay for the trumpet. The gun was fired in self-defence. Everyone is innocent, the swan is honest, the debt is paid, the storekeeper is rich, and the case is dismissed.'

A cheer went up from the crowd. The warden looked sulky. The policeman looked glum. But the storekeeper was beaming. He was a happy man. He felt that justice had been done.

'I have an announcement,' he said. 'I am only going to keep just enough of this money to pay for the stolen trumpet and the repair bills for my store. All the rest of the money will be given to a good cause if I can think of just the right one. Can anyone think of a worthy cause that needs money?'

'The Salvation Army,' suggested a woman.

'No,' said the storekeeper.

'The Boy Scouts?' suggested a boy.

'No,' said the storekeeper.

'The American Civil Liberties Union?' suggested a man.

'Nope,' said the storekeeper. 'Nobody has thought of just the right place for me to send this money.'

'How about the Audubon Society?' asked a little fellow whose nose looked like the beak of a bird.

'Great! You've got it!' cried the storekeeper. 'A bird has been very good to me, and now I want to do something for birds. The Audubon

Society is kind to birds. I want this money to be used to help birds. Some birds are in real trouble. They face extinction.'

'What's extinction?' asked Alfred Gore. 'Does it mean they stink?'

'Certainly not,' said the storekeeper. 'Extinction is what happens when you're extinct – when you don't exist any more because there are no others like you. Like the passenger pigeon and the eastern Heath Hen and the Dodo and the Dinosaur.'

'The Trumpeter Swan was *almost* extinct,' said the game warden. 'People kept shooting them, like this crazy storekeeper. But now they are making a comeback.'

The storekeeper glared at the warden.

'*I'll* say they're making a comeback,' he said. 'The swan that was just here *came back* to Billings with four thousand four hundred and twenty dollars and seventy-eight cents and gave it all to me. I call that making a very good comeback. I can't imagine where he *got* all that money. It's a mighty funny thing.'

The storekeeper went back into his music store, the policeman went back to the station house, the judge went back to the courthouse, the game warden walked off down the street toward the hospital, and Alfred Gore, who was still thirsty, continued his journey to the candy store. All the rest of the people wandered away.

At the hospital, the old cob lay peacefully in bed thinking beautiful thoughts. He felt thankful to be alive and relieved to be out of debt.

It was getting dark. Many of the patients in the hospital were asleep already. A nurse came into the cob's room to open his window.

When she came back a few minutes later to take the cob's temperature and give him a back rub, the bed was empty – the room was deserted. The cob had jumped out of the window, spread his broad wings, and headed for home through the cold night sky. He flew all night, crossed the mountains, and arrived home soon after daylight, where his wife was waiting for him.

'How did it go?' she asked.

'Very well,' he said. 'An extraordinary adventure. I was shot at, just as you predicted. The storekeeper pointed a gun at me and fired. I felt an agonizing pain in my left shoulder – which I've always considered the more beautiful of my two shoulders. Blood gushed from my wound in torrents, and I sank gracefully to the sidewalk, where I handed over the money and thus regained my honour and my decency. I was at death's door. A great multitude of people gathered. Blood was everywhere. I became faint and passed out with dignity in front of all. The police arrived – dozens of them. Game wardens flocked to the scene in great numbers, and there was a tremendous argument about the money.'

'How did you know all this if you were unconscious?' asked his wife.

'My dear,' said the cob, 'I wish you wouldn't interrupt me when I am telling the story of my trip. Seeing my grave condition, someone in the crowd summoned an ambulance, and I was taken to the hospital, where I was put to bed. I looked very beautiful lying there, my black bill contrasting with the snowy white sheets. Doctors and nurses attended me and comforted me in my hour of suffering and pain. You can judge how serious my wound was when I tell you that one of the doctors examined it and said it was superficial.'

'It doesn't look bad to me,' said his wife. 'I think you just got nicked. If it had been bad, you couldn't have flown back so soon. Anyway, superficial or not, I'm glad to see you home safe. I always miss you when you're gone. I don't know why, but I do.'

And with that, she placed her head across his neck and gave him a slight nudge. Then they had breakfast and went for a swim in an open place in the frozen lake. The cob pulled his Band-Aid off and threw it away.

21. The Greening Spring

LOUIS and Serena were more in love than ever. When spring came, they flew north, Louis wearing his trumpet and his slate and his chalk pencil and his medal, Serena wearing nothing at all. Now that he no longer had to work and earn, Louis felt a great sense of relief. No more would he have to carry a moneybag around his neck.

The two swans flew high and fast, ten thousand feet above the earth. They arrived at last at the little pond in the wilderness where Louis had been hatched. This was his dream – to return with his love to the place in Canada where he had first seen the light of day. He escorted Serena from one end of the pond to the other and back again. He showed her the tiny island where his mother's nest had been. He showed her the log Sam Beaver had been sitting on when Louis had pulled his shoelace because he couldn't say ko-hoh. Serena was enchanted. They were in love. It was spring. The frog was waking from his long sleep. The turtle was coming to life again after his nap. The chipmunk felt the warm air, soft and kind, blow through the trees, just as it did in that springtime when Louis's father and mother had visited the pond to nest and raise their young.

The sun shone down, strong and steady. Ice was melting; patches of open water appeared on the pond. Louis and Serena felt the changing world, and they stirred with new life and rapture and hope. There was a smell in the air, a smell of earth waking after its long winter. The trees were putting out tiny green buds, the buds were swelling. A better, easier time was at hand. A pair of Mallard Ducks flew in. A sparrow with a white throat arrived and sang, 'Oh, sweet Canada, Canada, Canada!'

Serena chose a muskrat lodge on which to build her nest. It was the right height above the water. The muskrats had built it of mud and sticks. Louis had hoped his wife might decide to make her nest in the same spot where his mother had built hers, but females are full of notions; they want their own way, pretty much, and Serena knew what she was doing. Louis was so delighted when he saw her begin to construct the nest, he didn't really care where it was. He raised his horn to his mouth and played the beginning of an old song called 'It's delightful to be married, to be-be-be-be, be-be-be-be married . . .' Then he helped by bringing a few pieces of coarse grass.

Rain or shine, cold or warm, every day was a happy day for the two swans. In time, the eggs were laid and the cygnets were hatched – four of them. The first sound the baby swans heard was the pure, strong sound of their father's trumpet.

'Oh, ever in the greening spring,' he played, 'By bank and bough retiring . . .'

Life was gay and busy and sweet in the little lonely pond in the north woods. Once in a while Sam Beaver would show up for a visit, and they would have great times together.

Louis never forgot his old jobs, his old friends, or his promise to the Head Man in Charge of Birds in Philadelphia. As the years went by, he and Serena returned each spring to the pond, nested, and had their young. And each year, at the end of summer, when the moult was over and the flight feathers grew back in and the cygnets were ready to try their wings, Louis took his family for a long pleasure trip across America. He led them first to Camp Kookooskoos, where he had saved the life of Applegate Skinner and won his medal. The camp would be closed for the season, but Louis liked to revisit it and wander around, remembering the boys and how he had earned his first hundred dollars as camp bugler.

Then the swans would fly to Boston, where the Swan Boat man always gave them a big welcome. Louis would polish up his horn, blow the spit out of it, and swim in front of the boats again, playing 'Row, row, row your boat,' and the people of Boston would hear the familiar sound of the trumpet of the swan and would flock to the Public Garden. Then the Boatman would treat Louis and Serena to a night at the Ritz Hotel, while the cygnets spent the night by themselves on the lake, watched over by the Boatman. Serena dearly loved the Ritz. She ate dozens of watercress sandwiches and gazed at herself in the mirror and swam in the bathtub. And while Louis stood and looked out of the window at the Public Garden down below, Serena would walk round and around, turning lights on and off for the fun of it. Then they would both get into the bathtub and go to sleep.

From Boston, Louis would lead his family to the Philadelphia Zoo and show them Bird Lake. Here, he would be greeted warmly by the Head Man in Charge of Birds. If the Zoo needed a young Trumpeter Swan to add to its collection of waterfowl, Louis would donate one of his cygnets, just as he had promised. In later years, Philadelphia was also the place where they would see Sam Beaver. Sam took a job with the Zoo just as soon as he was old enough to go to work. He and Louis always had a great time when they got together. Louis would get out his slate, and they would have a long talk about old times.

After visiting Philadelphia, Louis would fly south with his wife and children so they could see the great savannas where alligators dozed in the swamp water and Turkey Buzzards soared in the sky. And then they would return home to spend the winter in the Red Rock Lakes of Montana, in the lovely, serene Centennial Valley, where all Trumpeter Swans feel safe and unafraid.

The life of a swan must be a very pleasant and interesting life. And of course Louis's life was particularly pleasant because he was a musician. Louis took good care of his trumpet. He kept it clean and spent hours polishing it with the tips of his wing feathers. As long as he lived, he felt grateful to his father, the brave cob who had risked his life in order to give him the trumpet he needed so badly. Every time Louis looked at Serena, he remembered that the sound of the trumpet was what had made her willing to become his mate.

Swans often live to be very old. Year after year, Louis and Serena returned in spring to the same small pond in Canada to raise their

family. The days were peaceful. Always, just at the edge of dark, when the young cygnets were getting sleepy, Louis would raise his horn and play taps, just as he used to do at camp long ago. The notes were sad and beautiful as they floated across the still water and up into the night sky.

One summer, when Sam Beaver was about twenty, he and his father were sitting in their camp in Canada. It was after supper. Mr Beaver was rocking in a chair, resting after a day of fishing. Sam was reading a book.

'Pop,' said Sam, 'what does "crepuscular" mean?'

'How should I know?' replied Mr Beaver. 'I never heard the word before.'

'It has something to do with rabbits,' said Sam. 'It says here that a rabbit is a crepuscular animal.'

'Probably means timid,' said Mr Beaver. 'Or maybe it means that it can run like the dickens. Or maybe it means stupid. A rabbit will sit right in the middle of the road at night and stare into your headlights and never get out of the way, and that's how a lot of rabbits get run over. They're stupid.'

'Well,' said Sam, 'I guess the only way to find out what "crepuscular" means is to look it up in the dictionary.'

'We haven't got a dictionary here,' said Mr Beaver. 'You'll have to wait till we get back to the ranch.'

Just then, over at the pond where the swans were, Louis raised his horn and played taps, to let his children know that the day had come to an end. The wind was right, and the sound carried across the swamp.

Mr Beaver stopped rocking.

'That's funny!' he said. 'I thought I heard the sound of a trumpet just then.'

'I don't see how you could,' replied Sam. 'We're alone in these woods.'

'I know we are,' said Mr Beaver. 'Just the same, I thought I heard a trumpet. Or a bugle.'

Sam chuckled. He had never told his father about the swans in the pond nearby. He kept their secret to himself. When he went to the pond, he always went alone. That's the way he liked it. And that's the way the swans liked it.

'What ever happened to your friend Louis?' asked Mr Beaver. 'Louis was a trumpeter. You don't suppose *he's* somewhere around here, do you?'

'He might be,' said Sam.

'Have you heard from him recently?' asked Mr Beaver.

'No,' replied Sam. 'He doesn't write any more. He ran out of postage stamps, and he has no money to buy stamps with.'

'Oh,' said Mr Beaver. 'Well, the whole business about that bird was very queer – I never did fully understand it.'

Sam looked across at his father and saw that his eyes had closed. Mr Beaver was falling asleep. There was hardly a sound to disturb the stillness of the woods.

Sam was tired and sleepy too. He got out his notebook and sat down at the table by the light of the kerosene lamp. This is what he wrote:

Tonight I heard Louis's horn. My father heard it, too. The wind was right, and I could hear the notes of taps, just as darkness fell. There is nothing in all the world I like better than the trumpet of the swan. What does 'crepuscular' mean?

Sam put his notebook away. He undressed and slid into bed. He lay there, wondering what 'crepuscular' meant. In less than three minutes he was fast asleep.

On the pond where the swans were, Louis put his trumpet away. The cygnets crept under their mother's wings. Darkness settled on woods and fields and marsh. A loon called its wild night cry. As Louis relaxed and prepared for sleep, all his thoughts were of how lucky he was to inhabit such a beautiful earth, how lucky he had been to solve his problems with music, and how pleasant it was to look forward to another night of sleep and another day tomorrow, and the fresh morning, and the light that returns with the day.

Extra!

Extra!

E. B. WHITE

The
Trumpet
of the
Swan

ABOUT THE AUTHOR

E. B. WHITE

1899 *Born 11 July in Mount Vernon, New York, USA*

1921 *Graduated from Cornell University*

1922 *Became a reporter for the* Seattle Times *newspaper*

1927 *Appointed a contributing editor to the* New Yorker
     magazine, where he met his wife, Katharine

1945 Stuart Little *published*

1952 Charlotte's Web *published*

1959 *Co-authored* The Elements of Style
     (a book for writers)

1970	The Trumpet of the Swan *published*
1971	*Awarded the National Medal for Literature*
1985	*Died at home in Maine, USA, on 1 October*

ABOUT THE ILLUSTRATOR — EDWARD FRASCINO

Edward Frascino has written and illustrated many children's books, including Rudyard Kipling's The Elephant's Child. *He is also a regular cartoonist for the* New Yorker – *an American review magazine well known for its illustrated covers and topical cartoons.*

WHERE DID THE
STORY COME FROM?

E. B. White started writing for children in the late 1930s, when a young niece asked for a story. He first published Stuart Little *in 1945, and then* Charlotte's Web *in 1952, followed by* The Trumpet of the Swan *in 1970.*

E. B. White said, 'I don't know how or when the idea for The Trumpet of the Swan *occurred to me. I guess I must have wondered what it would be like to be a Trumpeter Swan and not be able to make a noise.'*

GUESS WHO?

A

*He didn't know what **mayonnaise** tasted like, but he thought fast. He cleaned his slate and wrote: 'One with. Eleven without.'*

B

*'I **know** you. You're the one that never said anything and used to pull my shoelaces.'*

C

*'I have **robbed** a store,' he said to himself. 'I have become a **thief**. What a miserable fate for a bird of my excellent character and high ideals! Why did I do this? What led me to commit this awful crime? My past life has been blameless – a model of good behaviour and correct conduct. I am by nature law-abiding. **Why, oh why did I do this?'**

ANSWERS: A) *Louis* B) *Sam* C) *Louis's father*

WORDS GLORIOUS WORDS!

Lots of words have several different meanings – here are a few you'll find in this Puffin book. Use a **dictionary** or look them up online to find other definitions.

chickadee

a small bird native to North America

idyllic

ideal, perfect

vigilant

to be alert, ready, or looking out for danger

migration

when birds or animals travel long distances to a different place when the seasons change

catastrophe

an event that causes great damage

disinclined

to be unwilling or reluctant, to not want to

sensation

a feeling, often intense

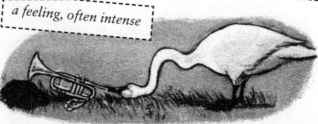

DID YOU KNOW?

E. B. White *began writing from a very early age – from the moment he learned to spell!*

E. B. White loved **sailing** *and named his boat* **'Martha'** *after his* **granddaughter**.

E. B. White lived on a **farm**, *and on that farm there was a barn that inspired many of his* **animal stories**.

QUIZ

Thinking caps on – *let's see how much you can remember! Answers are at the bottom of the opposite page. (No peeking!)*

1 *What animal does Sam protect the swans from?*

a) *A cat*

b) *Another swan*

c) *A dog*

d) *A fox*

2 *What did Louis's mother first notice about his father?*

a) *His feathers*

b) *His beak*

c) *His voice*

d) *His sense of humour*

3 *What does Jennie think is a catastrophe?*

a) *Not being able to have a picnic because of rain*

b) *Burning her toast*

c) *Losing one of her shoes at the park*

d) *Losing her favourite pen*

4 *What song does Louis play in the Ritz Hotel?*

a) *'Heartbreak Hotel'*

b) *'There's a Small Hotel'*

c) *'Hotel California'*

d) *The American National Anthem*

5 *Where does Sam realize he wants to work?*

a) *In the zoo*

b) *At the park*

c) *In a school*

d) *In an ice-cream van*

LOUIS SAYS:
'They say that falling in love is wonderful ...'

ANSWERS: 1) d 2) c 3) a 4) b 5) a

ALL ABOUT SWANS

The **Trumpeter Swan** is the largest waterbird in North America. It was **nearly extinct** in the early twentieth century, but today there are lots of them once more.

Male swans are **cobs**, female swans are **pens** and baby swans are **cygnets**.

Swans are **monogamous**, which means that once they choose a mate they stay with them for life.

In England, the Queen is regarded as the owner of every mute swan on the Thames, and employs an official **Swan Keeper** to be in charge of them. Every year a ceremony to count their numbers is held, called **Swan Upping!**

Most people think of swans as **white birds**, but that's only true in the northern hemisphere. In the southern hemisphere, in countries such as **New Zealand** and **Australia**, swans have **black feathers!**

MAKE AND DO

How to **draw a swan**

1   *Draw a small circle for the swan's head and the shape of its beak. Then draw an egg shape for the body, leaving room between each shape for the swan's long neck.*

2 *Draw the beak, but remember that swans do not have big beaks, so it should only go about halfway up the swan's forehead.*

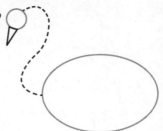

3 *Now put in a large patch by the eye for the swan's eye-marking. Draw the swan's long, graceful neck, joining the head to its body, but make it a little bit fatter in the middle.*

4 *Draw some lovely ruffled feathers on the swan's body, and do the same for its wing and tail.*

5 *Then colour in! For a Trumpeter Swan you'll need only two colours: black and orange. Give the swan an orange or black beak and orange legs. Finished!*

IN THIS YEAR

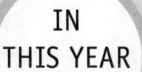

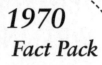

1970
Fact Pack

What else was happening in the world when this Puffin book was published?

The era of **global travel** begins when the first **jumbo jet** – the Boeing 747 – lands at Heathrow airport.

Many **coal mines close** because the need for coal in Britain is no longer as great as it had once been.

Conservative MP **Edward Heath** becomes the **Prime Minister** of the United Kingdom.

PUFFIN WRITING TIP

Listen to your favourite piece of music and then write about what you imagine as it plays.

LOUIS SAYS:

'Safety is all well and good: I prefer freedom.'

FROM THE ARCHIVE

Here is a *letter* written many years ago by **E. B. White** to all his fans.

Dear Reader

I receive many letters from children and can't answer them all – there wouldn't be time enough in a day. That is why I am sending you this printed reply to your letter. I'll try to answer some of the questions that are commonly asked.

Where did I get the idea for STUART LITTLE and for CHARLOTTE'S WEB? Well, many years ago I went to bed one night in a railway sleeping car, and during the night I dreamed about a tiny boy who acted rather like a mouse. That's how the story of Stuart Little got started.

As for CHARLOTTE'S WEB, I like animals and my barn is a very pleasant place to be, at all hours. One day when I was on my way to feed the pig, I began feeling sorry for the pig because, like most pigs, he was doomed to die. This made me sad. So I started thinking of ways to save a pig's life. I had been watching a very big grey spider at her work and was impressed by how clever she was at weaving. Gradually I worked the spider into the story that you know, a story of friendship and salvation on a farm. Three years after I started writing it, it was published.

I don't know how or when the idea for THE TRUMPET OF THE SWAN occurred to me. I guess I must have wondered what it would be like to be a Trumpeter Swan and not be able to make a noise.

Sometimes I'm asked how old I was when I started to write, and what made me want to write. I started early – as soon as I could spell. In fact, I can't remember any time in my life when I wasn't busy writing. I don't know what caused me to do it, or why I enjoyed it, but I think children often find pleasure and satisfaction in trying to set their thoughts down on paper, either in words or in pictures. As I grew older, I found that writing can be a way of earning a living.

Are my stories true, you ask? No, they are imaginary tales, containing fantastic characters and events. In *real* life, a family doesn't have a child who looks like a mouse; in *real* life, a spider doesn't spin words in her web. In *real* life, a swan doesn't blow a trumpet. But real life is only one kind of life – there is also the life of the imagination. And although my stories are imaginary, I like to think that there is some truth in them, too – truth about the way people and animals feel and think and act.

Thank you all for your wonderful letters – I love to get them even though I cannot answer each one personally.

Yours sincerely

E. B. White

HOW MANY HAVE YOU READ?

stories that last a lifetime

Animal tales

- [ ] The Trumpet of the Swan
- [ ] Gobbolino
- [ ] Tarka the Otter
- [ ] Watership Down
- [ ] A Dog So Small

War stories

- [ ] Goodnight Mister Tom
- [ ] Back Home
- [ ] Carrie's War

Magical adventures

- [ ] The Neverending Story
- [ ] Mrs Frisby and the Rats of NIMH
- [ ] A Wrinkle in Time

Unusual friends

- [ ] Stig of the Dump
- [ ] Stuart Little
- [ ] The Borrowers
- [ ] Charlotte's Web
- [ ] The Cay

Real life

- [ ] Roll of Thunder, Hear My Cry
- [ ] The Family from One End Street
- [ ] Annie
- [ ] Smith

A PUFFIN BOOK

stories that last a lifetime

Ever wanted a friend who could take you to magical realms, talk to animals or help you survive a shipwreck? Well, you'll find them all in the **A PUFFIN BOOK** collection.

A PUFFIN BOOK will stay with you **forever**. Maybe you'll read it again and again, or perhaps years from now you'll suddenly **remember** the moment it made you **laugh** or **cry** or simply see things **differently**. Adventurers **big** and **small**, rebels out to **change** their world, even a mouse with a **dream** and a spider who can spell – these are the characters who make **stories** that last a **lifetime**.

Whether you love animal tales, war stories or want to know what it was like growing up in a different time and place, the **A PUFFIN BOOK** collection has a story for you – you just need to decide where you want to go next . . .